THE AMULET'S CURSE

BY

AYN O'REILLY WALTERS

Grosvenor House
Publishing Limited

This book is published by
Grosvenor House Publishing Ltd
Link House
140 The Broadway, Tolworth, Surrey, KT6 7HT.
www.grosvenorhousepublishing.co.uk

A CIP record for this book
is available from the British Library

ISBN 978-1-80381-126-0
eBook ISBN 978-1-80381-127-7

PROLOGUE

The fleshy mortal,
one of three,
shall nay home to nest,
shall never be free.

2014

CHAPTER 1

Life was returning to normal for the Pritchard children following their recent adventure and were settling back into the routine of family life. William had turned 17 and continued to do well in his studies, and 13-year-old Isabel was now in year eight and spent her Sunday mornings working with a local charity by helping out in a flower shop just down the road from her home. Her favourite subjects were history and music. She played the violin, and loved being on the school swim team, just like her father when he was at university. She still didn't know what she wanted to do when she finished school but thought of studying history at university. After all, her travels through the trees would make learning much easier and more fun as her in-depth knowledge of history would surely earn her top marks. But for now she was content getting through secondary school and passing her grades. She spent just about all of her spare time with Jess, her best friend, whom she had met in primary school. They were inseparable and Jess seemed to fill the void of her father's absence, whom she missed so desperately. Jess had a passion for music and was a gifted pianist. Often Isabel tagged along to Jess's music recitals, and they performed duets at school concerts. She was there to encourage Jess when she felt nervous performing her solo numbers. They declared that they would be best friends for the rest of their lives, and nothing would ever separate them.

On Sunday mornings when Isabel worked at her local flower shop, she got to know the locals very well and she loved seeing the joy on their faces when she made up their bouquets of flowers. Lilies, chrysanthemums, orchards, tulips and freesias filled the shop with colour. When the shop door opened, the sweet smell of jasmine made Isabel think of the scented flowers that filled her own garden.

The Pritchard family had recently bought a lovely home in Richmond, a lively borough just outside London on the River Thames. For the first time, they had a big garden and Isabel filled it with all sorts of colourful shrubs and flowers. The windows at the front of the house had window boxes and every spring Isabel planted daffodils. Her mum was happy for her to do as she pleased and the whole garden looked lovely. However, one thing was missing that you would usually find in a garden. There were no trees. After her travels through the trees in Bishop's Park, Isabel had a profound dislike of trees, especially big oaks. She used to think the big oaks in Bishop's Park looked lovely in the summer as they swayed back and forth in the gentle wind. In autumn she would watch the leaves turn golden to brown as they fell from the branches onto the dewy grass on her way to school in the morning. Something so wonderful and pretty that gave life to the small animals that made the trees their home now became an aspect of nature she absolutely loathed. She hoped that one day she might overcome this feeling of dread and fear, but in the meantime, it was the sweet-smelling flowers that made her happy.

Early one Sunday morning, Isabel went about her usual business of watering the plants in the shop. She swept up the leaves and petals from the floor and scooped them into a rubbish bag. While she tidied up the shop, she wondered what Mother would be cooking for dinner that evening.

When she finished, Isabel grabbed her coat and headed for the door, saying goodbye to the owner of the shop, Mrs Petunia, on her way out. Of course, Mrs Petunia wasn't her real name, but everybody called her that because she loved petunias and personally delivered them to the hospital and local care homes. She had done this for almost 20 years and one day as she dropped off the flowers at the hospital, a little boy was visiting his sick brother. He bumped into Mrs Petunia, and her flowers fell to the floor. The little boy helped pick them up and loved how the colours burst from the stems. He asked the woman the names of the flowers and she told him they were petunias. When the boy had finished helping pick up the flowers, he said "Goodbye, Mrs Petunia" and darted back into his brother's room. And so the name Mrs Petunia had stuck.

When Isabel opened the shop door to leave, a big cold gust of wind blew in and it made her shiver. She pulled the door against the heavy wind and slammed it shut. When she turned and took her first steps, she felt a tap on her shoulder. She ignored it, thinking it was just the wind. Another tap followed, although this tap felt more like a push or a shove. It almost pushed her into the door, and she quickly spun around. Nobody was there. She stood on the step and looked left and right down the street and all she saw was an old lady pushing a shopping cart. The feeling of being pushed frightened her, for she knew it wasn't really a gust of wind. Normally Isabel walked the 15-minute trip home, but today she decided to catch the bus, so she hurriedly walked across the road and waited at the bus stop. She was relieved to see the Number 33 in the distance rumbling down the road and she began to feel safe again. On the bus she sat behind a little girl and her mother. The little girl turned around and gave Isabel a steely glare. Isabel winked at the girl and cheekily poked her tongue out. The little girl grinned sheepishly and nestled into her mother's arms. *How cute*! thought Isabel.

Arriving at home, Isabel hung her coat and bag and found Mother in the kitchen.

"Ooooh... what's for dinner?" she asked as she gave her mother a big hug.

"Oh, just a little dish I'm whipping up."

"Homemade lasagne. My favourite!" squealed Isabel. "You know that I love you more and more each..."

"...Each and every time I cook your favourite meals." Mother laughed.

There was no doubt about Mother's cooking. She cooked pancakes for breakfast and prepared banquets for dinner. No matter how busy the Pritchards were, they always made sure they were home in the evenings to have their family meals together.

"How was your day?" Mother asked.

"Pretty quiet. Although I had the strangest feeling that I was followed home."

"Oh dear," replied Mother.

"Oh no, it's okay, really." Isabel saw the concern on Mother's face. "It was just a weird feeling. Nobody actually followed me home. I guess I'm just a bit tired."

"Well, that's a relief." Mother sighed.

Isabel decided not to tell Mother about the strange shove she felt as she left the shop. It would worry her to no end and after what the family had been through, the last thing any of them needed was worry. Isabel convinced herself that her mind was playing tricks on her because she felt tired. Since she last travelled through the trees, she had become quite jumpy at the slightest thing and didn't much like being on her own.

That evening, the family sat down to a delicious lasagne together. They chatted about their day. William talked about his studies and how pressured he felt in preparing for his final school exams as he needed straight A's to get into medical school. However, every time he thought about life at university, he felt incredibly sad that his dad couldn't be there to help him, to answer all the complex questions about the human body, and to have someone to spend time with and chat endlessly about sport and all the stuff that boys and their dads talk about.

"Have you everything ready for school tomorrow?" Mother asked Isabel.

"There's no homework. We have the excursion to Kew Gardens."

"Of course! I completely forgot. That sounds lovely."

"I told Mrs Petunia I'd bring some flower seeds for the shop."

"My darling," replied Mother. "Always thinking of others."

The following morning, Isabel arrived at school and lined up with the rest of her class in the courtyard as they waited for the bus to take them to Kew Gardens. Jess sprinted into the school grounds, late as usual, and ran to the line. Her hair was bobbing up and down and her laces were untied, but she managed not to trip over them as she ran, which made her look rather funny trying to navigate her way around the laces as they flopped this way and that on the ground. The girls were so close that Jess often popped into the flower shop every so often and the two chatted about everything. They chose the same classes at school so they could sit next to each other. Isabel never told Jess about the family's time travel through the trees, for it was a family secret that must remain that way forever, or so she thought.

"Izzy!" said Jess, puffing and panting. The bus had arrived, and the children all hopped on.

"You're always late!" Isabel laughed. "Don't you have an alarm?"

"Oh yeah, Mum's my alarm! She comes in and shakes the bed and I say *I'm coming* and then when she leaves, I turn over and go back to sleep. And you know how much I love to sleep."

"How could I forget! Remember that time you missed the bus for swimming trials last year? I had to pretend that you were actually on the bus so you wouldn't get detention."

"Ha ha," laughed Jess. "I remember that! Mum had to drive me to the aquatic centre, and I had to sneak in and pretend I'd just finished the first race."

After a noisy bus ride on the oldest school bus that possibly existed in the whole of England, the children had arrived at Kew Gardens. At the entrance gate, the teacher ushered the children through and followed the path towards the glasshouse. As Isabel stood on the steps outside the glasshouse, she remembered the Crystal Palace at the Great Exhibition of 1851 and how similar they looked. Both had a big glass dome in the centre and hundreds of panels of glass on either side of the big rectangular structure. However, the glasshouse at Kew Gardens was dwarfed in size compared to the gigantic Crystal Palace that Prince Albert had painstakingly commissioned. A gust of warm air surged into Isabel's face when the doors were opened. The glasshouse was filled with tropical plants from the world's warmest climates and the room was warm and humid from the underground heating system that had been installed in the early 19th century.

"Hello there!" came a nearby voice. "Pop yourselves over here." The children shuffled slowly towards the woman. "Hurry up now. We have a lot to learn," said the voice enthusiastically.

A woman with an apron around her waist and a pair of secateurs in her hand stood at a bench. The children mingled around the bench with their pens and paper and the woman introduced herself as Mrs Struber.

"Good morning, class, I'm Mrs Struber and the building you are in is called 'Temperate House'. It was built in 1862, is 628 feet long and houses over 1500 species of plants." She continued telling the class about the tropical plants and how they came to be in Kew Gardens.

"When Joseph Banks travelled the world on the *Endeavour* with James Cook in 1768, he brought back thousands of species of plants and seeds, many of which were planted right here," hollered Mrs Struber. "The enormous glass and iron structure was not only the largest greenhouse in the world, but home to plants and trees from Australia, the Pacific Islands and the Americas to name just a few."

As the children stood there, they looked utterly bored. Some fidgeted with their smart phones, some looked out of the glasshouse windows behind Mrs Struber and watched the gardeners carrying plants in wheelbarrows around the pathways, and some children just stood silently, probably counting down the days until the end of term or wondering what they were planning to do on the weekend.

By lunchtime the class had made their way over to the Orangery Cafe, a long white building with rows of arched windows along the front. The children sat at tables scattered around the cafe and ate their lunch from their backpacks. As they ate their lunch, they chatted in little groups while Mrs Struber ate her lunch with the class teacher. When lunch had finished, the children were free to roam the gardens and meet back at the entrance to return to school.

They had one hour to find a plant and research all they could as part of their homework.

Isabel and Jess decided to walk over to the other side of the gardens and see what they could find. It was a beautiful day to be outside, for the sky was blue and the flowers in Kew Gardens were in full bloom. It was lovely to walk past rows of yellow daffodils as people wandered around the gardens chatting happily.

The pair walked around the gardens arm in arm. Jess pulled a bag of sweets from her purse, and they ate them as they walked. They stopped when they found themselves in front of a big red house. The grand house was three storeys tall, had more than 20 windows and no less than 15 chimney pots on the roof. It was massive and looked even bigger as it stood alongside the banks of the River Thames. When the sun shone over the house, it changed in colour to a bright terracotta.

"What's that over there?" asked Jess.

"Not sure. Looks like a big old house."

"A bit odd in the middle of a park. I wonder if anyone lives there."

"I wouldn't think so," said Isabel. "Maybe a few hundred years ago."

"It's quite beautiful, don't you think?"

"Yes, it's very pretty. Shall we have a look?"

The two girls walked up to the grand house and stepped inside. A rope intertwined on metal poles had cordoned off sections of the house. It looked somewhat like a museum and the girls walked into the first room on the left, which had obviously been used as a library in a bygone era. A mahogany desk sat in the corner with a big leather chair behind it. The room smelled old and musty. Isabel noticed some paintings on the walls. One grand painting showed a regal-looking man wearing a military uniform while other smaller paintings showed a mother and her children sitting around her. Judging from the clothes they were wearing, Isabel assumed the paintings were at least 200 years old. The little boys wore knickerbockers, and the men wore tights. They had enormous white wigs perched on their heads.

Isabel pored her eyes admiringly over all of the faces in the paintings. She was fascinated with all of the people, and when she slowly moved past the painting, it was as though they were also looking back at her. In the far corner of the room, another painting caught her attention. She walked closer to it and, all of a sudden, she began trembling. The man in the painting wore long red robes and a gold crown sat neatly on his head. It was clear he was a king. He proudly showed off the shiny rings on his fingers as he clutched the sceptre. He looked very important, and he held his head high. Isabel stopped and stared. There was something about this painting that felt odd. She couldn't put her finger on it, so she stood back and looked at it from a different angle.

"Oh my!" she shrieked.

"What is it?" asked Jess, startled.

"Oh my!" was all Isabel could say. She was in complete and utter shock. She took a closer look and there it was again, as clear as daylight.

As Isabel stood there in shock, and Jess was wondering what on earth was going on, a man entered the room.

"Who are you?" he bellowed. "What are you doing in here?" With his hands on his hips, he waited for an answer. Isabel was in so much shock she didn't even notice the man standing there.

"Errr... we were just leaving," stammered Jess as she grabbed hold of Isabel's hand and pulled her away from the picture. "Come on, Izzy, let's go."

The girls scurried past the man and out the front door.

"What was that about?" asked Jess.

"I'm sorry, Jess, I have to get home. I can't explain it. I just need to go."

The girls ran through the gardens and back into the glasshouse. As soon as they were inside, they stopped to catch their breath.

"Right," said Jess. "You can tell me what's going on later. The nearest exit is through those doors and straight back to the bus."

"I can't wait for the bus!" cried Isabel. "I have to get home now! I need to see William!"

Isabel ran through the glasshouse and pushed the doors open at the other end.

Jess ran behind her. "Wait!" she said. "We have to wait for the class! We can't just leave!"

Isabel ignored Jess and kept running towards the exit. She ran around a tree and literally ran into a gardener.

"I'm really sorry," said Isabel as the gardener looked nonplussed.

"Look where you're going," he muttered and walked off with his wheelbarrow.

Isabel continued running and soon started to feel tired. Her legs felt heavy, and she began dragging her feet. She ran past a tree and tripped over its roots, ending up face down on the ground. Jess soon caught up with her. "Are you okay?" she asked, puffing and panting.

"I'm okay, I just tripped over these stupid roots. Stupid tree."

"Let me help," said Jess. "Here, give me your hand and I'll pull you up."

As Jess tried to heave Isabel up from the ground, she also fell down and burst out laughing.

"It's not funny!" Isabel was quite upset that Jess thought the whole incident was so entertaining.

"Sorry," replied Jess. "I know you need to get home. Come on, let's go."

Around Isabel's neck was a small vial of liquid which was given to her by Mother, who instructed her to take it everywhere she went. The liquid was a very special potion that Mother had created. It was the only potion she had made since she went through the trees as a young girl and decided to live a normal life as a mortal. Isabel and William didn't need magic potions to travel through the trees, but Mother often wondered how long the trees would be open for the children to travel through. When William couldn't get back home from 1851 because Raven had wickedly removed his tree, Mother wasted no time in ensuring the safety of her children. So she made up her own spell and the potion was created. If the children ever got stuck without their tree, it could be used to travel. Isabel carried the vial around her neck and although she never used it, she felt safe knowing that it would always be there, just in case.

Isabel didn't notice that the vial of liquid had cracked for she was too preoccupied with what she had seen at the big red house. Jess grabbed Isabel's arm, and when the girls managed to stand up, Jess placed her hands on the tree to balance herself.

Isabel eventually found her feet, and when she stood up, she brushed the dirt and grass from her trousers.

"Right. Let's get out of here," Isabel said as she scooped her backpack up off the ground.

When Jess didn't respond, Isabel looked around.

"Jess?"

She looked here and there, but Jess wasn't anywhere.

"Jess!" hollered Isabel. "Jess! Where are you?"

Where is she? she wondered as she looked around the gardens. *She can't have gone far*.

How strange, thought Isabel. Then she realised the collar of her top was damp. She quickly pulled the chain from under her top and opened her hands. The vial was broken, and small shards of glass glistened in her hand. The liquid was all gone.

"Nooooooo! No... no... no... no!!!" was the only word Isabel could speak when she looked up and saw the tree. She then realised that Jess had travelled. To where, she had no clue. All she knew was that she had to find Jess and bring her home. She could be anywhere, in any century. What a predicament! She had to find Jess, who had no knowledge of travelling through the trees and who would be absolutely distraught by now. Isabel could go through the same tree and bring her home, but what if something awful happened and she couldn't get back? She would never be able to see her mother again and her family would never know what had happened to her.

Regardless of the danger she was faced with, she knew what she had to do.

CHAPTER 2

Isabel opened her eyes and found herself lying on a patch of soft grass. She had no clue where she was, and when she sat up and looked around, everything looked the same, except she was wearing a lovely gown. Looking in the distance, she saw the big red house exactly as it was when she snuck in with Jess. She began walking towards the house and saw a little boy playing in the garden. He must have been about 10 for he was playing with wooden dolls dressed as soldiers.

Isabel walked along the grass. Her beautiful gown, yellow in colour, almost looked like a big ballooned wedding dress. Unlike the women whose gowns went all the way down to their shoes, Isabel's dress hung just below her knees and a big ribbon was tied neatly around the back of her waist. Under the top layer of her dress, whale bone held the shape of the dress in position, and it felt tight and uncomfortable around her chest. She wore dainty little slippers on her feet, the same colour as the yellow gown, with a robe over her shoulders.

"Pow pow," said the little boy as he aimed the soldiers towards each other. Isabel stopped and watched him.

"You're dead!" he muttered and thrashed the soldiers about. Then a young girl came running out of the house towards the boy.

"George! Mama said it's time for tea. You must come inside at once!"

The girl stood on the grass waiting for the young boy. She didn't look much older than him, probably a year or so, and she had dark curly hair tied in ringlets that hung neatly over her shoulders. She, too, was wearing a dress similar to Isabel's, although hers was made of pure silk, and it glimmered under the sun.

The boy scooped up his soldiers. "I'm coming, Augusta," he cried and scurried off.

Isabel walked up to the big red house and peered inside the front window. It was the room that she and Jess had walked into before they were ushered out by the man. The room looked the same; the big old desk was there, although it was now sitting in the middle of the room instead of the corner. Isabel walked around the side of the house and looked through another window. The room was empty. Just then she heard a splash, and all of a sudden, a voice cried out. It sounded like someone was in trouble. Isabel spun around and ran back to the front of the house. The little boy was nowhere to be seen.

"Help!" came the voice again.

Isabel ran towards a group of trees where she found a pond and noticed two arms thrashing about in the water.

"Oh gosh!" She sprinted over to the pond and jumped in. The boy who was playing with his soldiers had fallen into the pond. Isabel grabbed hold of him and pulled him up to the surface. The boy became limp, and his arms fell to his sides. Isabel dragged him over the side, but her dress was heavy and her robe, which was drenched with water, kept pulling her back under. She tugged at it furiously and pulled it off, then rolled the boy over the edge of the pond and lay him flat on the grass.

The boy was not moving, and his face was turning blue. For the first time ever, Isabel put her swimming training skills into practice. She tilted his head back and placed her mouth over his. She pinched his nose very slightly and blew into his mouth. *How many times?* she wondered. *That's it, five times.* Isabel was so preoccupied with saving the boy she didn't notice a gardener had also heard his screams. He dropped his rake and by the time he made it to the pond, Isabel had started chest compressions. She pushed her hands down onto his chest and began pumping. "One two three, one two three," she repeated over and over again. "Come on! Come on!" she cried. The gardener didn't know what to think. He knelt down next to Isabel and waited, willing the young boy to make it through. The boy lay still, so Isabel began the process all over again while the gardener just stared at her in sheer confusion at the goings-on of which he had never seen before.

Then all of a sudden, the boy coughed. She sat him up and slapped his back several times. A big gulp of water exploded from the boy's mouth, and he began gasping. Isabel threw her arms around him and held him tight as he began crying. "It's alright," she said. "You're okay. You just went for a little swim!"

"Mama," cried the boy as his cheeks returned to a pinkish hue.

The gardener scooped up the boy and they ran to the house with the boy still crying from the utterly frightening experience he'd just been through.

Isabel grabbed hold of his hand. "Come on, I'll take you to your mama. Everything will be alright."

The adrenaline coursed throughout Isabel's body. Her heart was thumping when she realised she had just saved someone's life.

"You're such a brave boy," she reassured him. "Almost home now."

When Isabel arrived at the house, she threw the big doors open and a butler came scurrying out of a nearby room. He was aghast to see someone burst through the doors and soon enough a flurry of activity was underway. Maids and butlers ran to the boy's aid and helped carry him into the house.

They pushed people out of the way as they entered a sitting room. A maid dressed in black shoved two sleeping dogs from a couch and propped up some pillows and the gardener gently lay him down. "Get the doctor!" came a voice. As Isabel stood in this grand sitting room dripping wet, all manner of things were happening. People were running in and out of the room asking what had happened, the man who ordered the doctor was now in the hallway shouting at someone, who then shouted at someone else, who ran out of a side door, jumped onto a horse and galloped off, with dust flying everywhere.

As blankets were wrapped around the little boy, a woman ran into the room. Her hair was tied up in a neat little bun on top of her head with delicate jewels and beads on either side. Her skin was as white as the pearls that hung around her neck. As she walked over to the little boy, her bright blue silk dress sashayed and lit up the room as the sun shone through the enormous windows.

"My dear boy" she sobbed as she bent down and held him close. Isabel knew that kind of hug, a loving tight embrace, for she had felt that with her own mother.

"Oh Mama," cried the boy. "I was drowning."

"Oh my goodness. What happened?" said the boy's mother as she kept him nestled under her breast. She looked around for someone to answer.

Everyone was looking at the gardener.

"He drowned" said he. "And this kind girl jumped into the pond and saved his life. Don't know what she did, but he was as good as dead, and she brought him back to life."

Then all of a sudden, everyone was looking at Isabel, who was standing in the corner of the room shivering and soaking wet.

"Are you alright, my darling?"

"Oh no, Mama, I am cold."

"Doctor is on his way. Not long to wait."

"I drowned in that pond," said the boy. "She saved me."

The boy poked his head up from the pillow and turned towards Isabel. The beautifully dressed woman walked over to Isabel and took her hands. "Thank you, from all of us." She smiled.

"You're v...v...very welcome," stammered Isabel. "Now that I see your son is alright, I do need to be on my way." Isabel began walking towards the door.

"But you are wet," said the woman. "My mistress will fetch some dry clothes. For now, you must wait until you are dry and comfortable enough to leave."

Isabel was handed a new dress, a fine dress made from silk that belonged to Augusta and she was grateful to change into the warm, dry clothes. As she changed, her thoughts quickly turned to Jess and the panic began to set in again. She had lost precious time helping the little boy and she couldn't spend any longer in this house. She had to find Jess.

When she passed the room to leave the house, the little boy tilted his head off the pillow. "Wait! I must say goodbye."

Isabel sat on the couch next to the boy.

"What is your name?" he asked.

"Isabel Pritchard."

"I am George, and my grandfather is King George II."

"Really?" asked a shocked Isabel. "That's a very important job. How old are you?" she asked.

"I'm 10. How old are you?"

"I'm 13," replied Isabel.

"You're almost an adult."

"Well, yes, I suppose I am, but now I'm just a teenager." She chuckled.

"Teenager?" said George, scrunching his little nose. "What is a teenager?"

"Perhaps," interrupted his mother, "it is a person who saves a life."

Isabel had to hold back for she almost burst out laughing. She covered her mouth with her hand as she enjoyed hearing the varying definitions of a teenager.

"Or..." came the maid's voice, "it is a person who looks young for their age."

"Not quite" replied Isabel. "A teenager is older than a child but younger than an adult."

The maids all looked at each other perplexed by this new word, *teenager*.

"Tell me, George, did you see another girl about my age, also a teenager, in these gardens?"

"Indeed I did!"

"Oh, that's great. Did you see where she went?"

George pointed to the window over to the other side of the gardens.

"Well then," said Isabel. "Thank you for your time. You're a very interesting, and important, person!"

"And you are rather peculiar."

"Why thank you!"

Isabel held out her hand and George gave it a gentle shake. When Isabel stepped out of the house, a horse roared towards her. She darted sideways, and several servants grabbed hold of the horse's reins as it slowed down. The doctor hopped off the horse and untied a black bag from the saddle. Clutching the little black bag, he charged into the house.

CHAPTER 3

After saving little George, Isabel raced out of the gardens and crossed the road. She had no idea how to find Jess. Walking down the main road, she passed rows of run-down dwellings. It occurred to her that she had been down this road before, and in the 21st century, they were in fact rows of shops, restaurants and cafes. Not that it helped in any way, but she assumed that walking the streets she was familiar with might help in finding her way around. Losing Jess *and* getting lost at the same time would be disastrous. Isabel found it quite difficult walking briskly in the big dress she was wearing, and she wished she could pop on a pair of jeans and trainers, but she didn't have any modern-day clothes which would draw negative attention. How could she explain herself in jeans, for all the girls and ladies around her were in dresses.

So she did the best she could and as she made her way down the end of the main road, the small houses faded away and she suddenly faced very unfamiliar territory. She found herself standing on a dirt road and all she could see ahead was farms and pastures. She realised she had to start asking people if they had seen Jess.

Standing on the side of the road, Isabel felt the earth trembling beneath her feet. It couldn't be that she was about to enter another time because she had not slapped her hands on a nearby tree. She looked towards the horizon and a big black object began to appear. It bobbed up and down, and as it drew closer, it became louder. Four horses galloped towards Isabel and a man sitting on top of a stagecoach pulled the rein hard and the horses slowed down. They neighed and pricked their pointy ears as they waited patiently. The man sat perched on the seat and Isabel stood back and waited for him to say something. Instead, the coach door creaked open, and a young man asked Isabel if she was troubled. He was very polite, taking off his hat and dipping his head towards Isabel as he spoke. Isabel knew to say very little and keep her head down, so she told him she was not in any trouble, that she was just looking for her friend. The young man introduced himself.

"I am John Bentley. *The* John Bentley of Hanover Square in London."

Isabel assumed he was an important person by the way he dressed and how polite he was. He had jet black hair slicked back behind his ears. She wondered whether she could trust him, but what option did she have? She thought it might be a wise idea to make a friend of him, so she described Jess to Mr Bentley. She told him Jess was about her own height with blonde hair and that she was also 13 years old.

Mr Bentley listened intently. "Hhhmmm. It is most unfortunate that I have not seen your friend on my travels. I am terribly sorry." He sighed.

"Oh." Isabel hung her head. "It's alright. I'm sure I'll find her."

"Perhaps I can offer you a ride somewhere. Is there any place you would like to go?"

Isabel wondered where on earth she would actually go if she accepted Mr Bentley's offer. Just the thought of it made her feel a little lonely.

"My coach is quite comfortable and has plenty of space. You could sit opposite me and tell me all about yourself."

Isabel peered into the carriage. It looked very comfortable indeed, for the seats were lined with dark blue velvet and little curtains hung from the sides of the windows. When Isabel glanced inside, sitting on John's lap was a book. At the top corner written in gold were the words '*Diary 1748*'. She tried her best not to look surprised.

Isabel had stumbled into the year 1748. It was the Georgian era and the birth of the Industrial Revolution. Britain's population grew rapidly from five million in 1700 to over nine million in 1800. Factories sprang up all over the country, new inventions were being made and England soon became a nation of great wealth and power. Men's fashion was rather unusual for they wore long coats and frilly white shirts with big frilly cuffs. Their knickerbockers stopped at their knees, with stark white tights and little black shoes with big gold buckles over the toes. Wigs were all the rage, not just for the ladies but the gents wore wigs too, often higher than the ladies. What a sight it was.

"Thank you Mr Bentley. It's very kind of you to offer, but I'm quite sure my friend is around here somewhere."

"Well then. I am quite certain you will find your friend. She can't have got very far without a horse."

Mr Bentley closed the coach door and placed his big black hat back on his head.

As the coach rolled away, he stuck his head out of the window.

"Remember," he yelled as the horses began to canter off, "I am John Bentley of Hanover Square! If you need help, you may call upon me at any time."

"Thank you!" shouted Isabel. She thought it was quite funny that she would be able to just head into the populated city of London and find Mr John Bentley by popping over to Hanover Square. In the 21st century one needed an actual address, or the chances would be near impossible. How simple life was in the old days; however, it was also a very hard life if you didn't have money. And Isabel had experienced the hard times first hand when she was forced to spend several weeks at the Bristol workhouse in 1851.

When the stagecoach was gone, Isabel turned around and then it dawned on her. She remembered being at a carnival when she was nine years old. Mother had taken her, Jess and William, and after they bought their tickets and joined the swarm of crowds, Mother told them that if they ever got lost, just head back to the place of origination and they would find each other.

"Yes!" she shouted. She clutched her dress as she ran all the way down the main road and past the houses. She didn't even notice that everyone had stopped to stare at her. Running back into the gardens and up a hill she found the tree she had travelled through. Sitting under the tree with her head in her hands was Jess.

"Jess! Jess! It's me! Izzy!" Isabel threw her arms around Jess and the girls hugged each other tightly.

"What's happening?" cried Jess. "I fell over and when I got up, you were gone and the park was different and when I went into the street, everyone was wearing silly clothes. Did you see that too? What's going on?"

Isabel calmed Jess down and began explaining the magic trees in Bishop's Park.

"Oh my, oh WOW!" was all Jess could say. "So, you're some sort of magic person then?"

"Sort of," replied Isabel. "My family can go back in time. It was something that I stumbled across, and it's been a mad journey ever since. Coming here was an accident too. I had a potion around my neck, and it broke when I fell over the roots of this tree. Then when you grabbed my hand to pull me up, the liquid was transferred to your hands and then you touched the tree. I'll tell you the whole story when we get home. It's a long one."

"You mean we've been best friends all along and you never told me," said Jess.

"I soooooo wanted to, really I did, but I couldn't. You wouldn't have believed me, and I couldn't take you with me anywhere to prove it in case we couldn't get back."

"Can we get back now?"

"Yes, but we have to go now. I need to see William to decide what to do next."

CHAPTER 4

When the girls travelled safely back to 2014, Jess stopped and looked down at her hands.

"Are we back?" she asked.

"Yes, I think we are. Oh yes, we're definitely home, see? We're wearing normal clothes again and look, there's the glasshouse."

Jess walked around the trunk of the big tree, looking at it from all manner of different angles. She dared not touch it again, for she wasn't sure where she would end up.

"Come on," said Isabel as she scooped her arm around Jess's. "Let's get home and I'll tell you everything."

When the girls arrived at Isabel's house, Jess poured two glasses of milk and they sat down at the kitchen table.

"I'm glad you're sitting down," said Isabel. "Because I need to tell you about my dad."

"But he died, didn't he?"

"Well, no. He's not dead at all. He's actually alive!"

"OMG! What did you just say?" Jess couldn't believe what she was hearing.

"He's stuck in 1851. He went back to rescue our cousin from a workhouse, and we found him in that same workhouse!"

Jess was clearly having trouble comprehending, for she just sat there completely dumbfounded.

"It's best if I just start from the beginning," said Isabel as she sipped her milk.

"I saw a glowing tree in Bishop's Park, where we used to live, and I put my hands on it. All of a sudden, I was transported to 1851."

"And?"

"I walked into the street and saw a man selling newspapers about Queen Victoria and the Great Exhibition."

"What's the Great Exhibition?"

"I'll get to that. I was so scared I ran back into the park and woke in my bed that evening. Mum was there, and she told me not to go back into the park."

"And you did?"

"Of course! I took William with me because he thought I was lying about the whole thing, then when we touched the tree, nothing happened. We started walking back home then I saw another tree glowing and we both ran over and touched it. Then all of a sudden, we were in 1945. It was VE Day and there were people celebrating in the streets. There were soldiers everywhere and street parties. It was really amazing."

"What did William think of it all?"

"Well, he realised I wasn't lying! He was like, wow! Couldn't believe it either. So anyway, we went back home and did some research on the park. We found out we were able to travel back to the year the tree was planted."

"Wow," said Jess. "What happened then?"

"We decided to return and ended up going through the first tree back to 1851. We were at the Great Exhibition and saw Queen Victoria and lots of famous people from that time, Charles Dickens, the Duke of Wellington, Charlotte Brontë and Lewis Carroll. Then we got caught for stealing and sent to a workhouse in Bristol. It was awful and we met a boy called George Fraser and found out he was actually our cousin who was sent there by his mum. George died trying to save William, but we found Dad there. He couldn't get back home because an accident happened and he lost his hand. You need both hands on the tree, so he's still there."

"Well, what's your dad doing in 1851 then?"

"He got away from the workhouse and is working as a doctor in London. He's also waiting to come home, but although we can go back and see him, Mum thinks it's best if we don't. Mum says messing with time can be very dangerous."

"I can understand that." Jess paused for a moment. "I just need to take this all in. I can't believe your dad's alive. It's incredible."

"We couldn't believe it either."

"Aren't you mad at your mum for telling you he was in an accident and died?"

"Not at all. We were just so happy Dad was alive. And besides, we understand she was trying to protect us. She's done a great job raising us on her own and she's so amazing. Everything she's been through... I wouldn't be that strong."

"Izzy, I'm so happy you found your dad alive."

CHAPTER 5

Isabel and Jess returned home and told William that she and Jess had just spent the afternoon in Georgian England, and he was rather upset with the girls. Although he knew Jess well and loved her like a little sister, it was crucial that *nobody* knew the secrets about their family. But now that Jess did know, there wasn't anything he could do about it except sit her down and have a very stern conversation on the utmost importance of keeping their secret. Isabel told William about the painting she saw at the big house in Kew Gardens. The man in the painting had the amulet around his neck.

"Oh my gosh," replied William. "It can't be! The amulet is here, in our house! Our mother has it!"

"I'm not wrong, Will," said Isabel. "I saw it with my own eyes."

"We need to find out who the man wearing it is."

"Right then. You said you saw a diary dated 1748. If you were in the Georgian era, that would mean a King George was on the throne."

"Here!" quipped Isabel. "I just googled Kew Gardens, and this came up."

William muttered as he read out loud. "Kew Palace... River Thames... Ah! King George II was on the throne, so you must have met his grandson."

"You mean *saved* his grandson from drowning," corrected Isabel.

"And by the way, that *was* Kew Palace you were in," said William.

"Well, that explains a lot!" replied Isabel.

William and Isabel scrolled through Isabel's phone and read about the history of Kew Palace in the Georgian era. They still didn't have a clue who was wearing the amulet and how it came to be because the amulet was safely tucked away in Mother's belongings.

The family ate dinner that evening in silence. Mother was feeling very unwell and began rambling. Isabel squeezed Mother's hand. "It's alright, Mum, we'll get you off to bed soon."

Then all of a sudden, Mother sat upright and in the most coherent manner said, "My dreams."

"What is it?" asked William. "Please tell us, Mum, it's really important."

"The amulet. Too much power."

"She must have heard us talking about it," said Isabel.

"We need to find it," replied William. He moved Mother's chair around to face him and looked directly into her eyes. "Mum, where is the amulet?"

"It's too powerful," she muttered and blankly stared out of the kitchen window.

"Oh my gosh. That's it!" cried William. "The amulet is making her ill. The amulet is causing all the headaches, the bad dreams, everything. We have to find it urgently."

"But we don't know where it is."

"Well then, we'll turn this house upside down until we find it."

The children looked everywhere. They must have looked behind every cupboard, inside every drawer, they even turned up every mattress and bed in the house. But it was no use. After spending an entire weekend searching the house, it was nowhere to be found. They realised that Mother must have accidentally thrown it away or simply lost it. No matter how many times they asked her, even when she was feeling okay, she just couldn't remember.

Upon returning from the 16th century when Drys gave Mother the talisman, she kept the amulet and talisman together. She wasn't sure where they belonged, who they belonged with or if they should remain with her. So she decided to keep them in a safe place away from her family. The less they knew about their whereabouts, the better. She wasn't even certain that her sister, Raven, was dead or alive for that matter. She always knew in her heart of hearts that if Raven turned up and demanded the stones, she would hand them over without hesitation. Her family were the most important people on Earth, and she would do whatever it took to protect them.

However, Mother forgot that Drys warned Raven that together, the talisman and amulet would be too powerful and like Drys had predicted, in Mother's hands, they were making her very ill.

In the days and weeks that followed after Mother returned home with the stones, she began having headaches. They went from the odd mild pain to very severe pain and dizziness. When she went to bed and fell asleep, the nightmares began. Every morning she wondered whether it was just the headaches that gave her the nightmares, but in the pit of her stomach, she had the awful notion that there was something more sinister going on. She dreamed the same nightmares over and over again, but she could never remember them when she woke up. She realised that something had to be done when she began muttering to herself. These mutterings turned into ramblings and when Isabel and William noticed these ramblings, they swiftly made an appointment to see a doctor, who carried out a multitude of tests, including brain scans. But alas, every test came back negative and after seeing several medical specialists, it was thought that Mother was descending into some sort of mania. On occasions, Mother seemed perfectly normal, then all of a sudden, she would either sit in a chair for hours on end in total silence or she would ramble on and on about nothing in particular. William spent months trying to find out what was wrong, and Isabel was heartbroken. Sometimes she took Mother to the flower shop thinking the flowers and plants might have a calming effect. However, things just got worse as the months went by.

A couple of weeks later, when Mother was sitting beside a window staring outside, she began rambling on about the books in the study. "They're too dusty," she kept repeating.

"It's alright, Mum," said William. "Don't worry, we will clean them."

"Too dusty," repeated Mother.

William held his mother close and hugged her. "Dust is okay, Mum," he whispered in her ear.

Then all of a sudden, Mother said, "The amulet will be ruined."

"What did you say?" asked a startled William.

Mother looked straight into William's eyes. "The amulet."

Then a flash went off in William's head. He raced into the study and stood in front of the walls that were filled with books. *It's got to be here! It has to be!*

It didn't take long for Isabel to hear thumping sounds from her bedroom. Maybe Mother had a fall. She ran into the study, and to her amazement, books were flying all over the room.

"William!" she shouted. "What's going on?" The floor was covered in books.

"The amulet! Mum said something about the amulet being ruined by the dust on the books."

"I found it!" he cried.

William pulled out a small leather pouch from behind a section of books and dusted it off. He opened it carefully and inside lay the both amulet and the talisman. He pulled out the amulet and, for a few moments, just stared at it. "Found you," he whispered.

William turned to Isabel. "Now we have to find out who is wearing this amulet and when the painting was done."

Isabel laughed. "Isn't that what Google's for?" Together they searched for Georgian kings on the iPad until they eventually found an image that was identical to the painting the girls saw at Kew Palace. Painted by Allan Ramsay in 1768, the picture on the internet showed the magnificent amulet with its sparkling gems around the neck of the king as William held the very same amulet in his hand at that moment. He looked at Isabel and she understood what that look meant. They had to return the amulet to King George III in 1768.

CHAPTER 6

In the year 600 AD, a mercenary arrived on the shores of England by ship from Scandinavia. It was a period of war in England, and he joined an army of English soldiers to drive out the Romans from overtaking England. When the war had finished, the mercenary wasn't sure what to do next. He didn't want to go back to his homeland, so he decided to stay in England and find a nice little village to settle in.

He walked through small villages filled with little houses made from huts and eventually ended up in a market village in Yorkshire and liked it, so he decided to stay a while. He had little money and no possessions, so finding an inn with a warm bed and a hot meal was something he could only dream of. The man's name was Edwin. His father, too, was a warrior and died when Edwin was a young boy. His mother had recently died in a rather unfortunate way. While collecting water from a nearby stream, she lost her footing and slipped into the freezing water. She could not swim back to the riverbank for the hypothermia quickly overcame her, and she drowned.

On a hot summer's day, the small Yorkshire village where Edwin decided to settle was unusually busy as people took the opportunity to enjoy the sun. Children played in fields while their parents enjoyed watching them as they relaxed under the shade of nearby trees. It was a far contrast from the freezing winters where families stayed inside their dark and dreary homes huddled around fireplaces to keep warm.

All of Edwin's travelling and walking had made him tired and worn out. He had lost much of his strength and had aged well beyond his years. As the afternoon sun got hotter, Edwin sat under a tree to rest. He pulled a leather pouch that was tied to his waist and drank the water from inside. He sipped it slowly, for fear of it running out and not being able to find a nearby well in which to refill it. This summer was particularly hot, and the rains were few and far between. As Edwin dozed off, his head drooped down to his chin and his arms began to relax by his side. The heat had made everyone in the village tired and Edwin fell into a deep sleep. When he woke from his sleep, the sun had gone, and a bright full moon lit up the sky. The stars twinkled from one end of the sky to the other, and as he looked up, he wondered how they got there and why they sparkled so brightly.

The village at night was quiet. The market traders had packed up their wares and returned home to their families. All Edwin could hear was the bleating of sheep in nearby fields. He stretched out his arms and let out a huge yawn. Then he stood up and realised something was not right. He had been robbed. His water pouch was gone along with the gold coin that was attached to a leather strap around his wrist. He wondered how someone could have the audacity to actually remove something from his wrist as he slept. He was even more angry at himself for falling asleep and allowing it to happen. He was a soldier after all, and soldiers were proud, fierce, and not to be messed with. He was enraged and was determined to find out who was so impudent as to rob a soldier. So he waited. He sat under the tree and waited until sunrise. He watched the villagers emerge from their little huts as they went about setting up their stalls for another day's trade at the market. He waited patiently until the locals began descending on the market as they chatted among each other, buying their food and placing the little packages in their baskets. That night, Edwin watched the villagers go about their usual business. It would be another two days until he found out who had stolen from him.

On the third day, a well-dressed man sauntered into the village with his wife. They bought fish, bread and malt, and his wife happily handed small pennies to the stall owners. As she moved closer towards Edwin, she raised her arm to flick her hair away from her face. Something caught Edwin's attention. In the sunlight, a gold coin glistened from her wrist. Edwin immediately stood up and followed the man and his wife through the village and back to their home. While all of the villagers lived in small wooden huts with only one room, this couple lived in a big house with half a dozen rooms. Edwin realised this was indeed a very important man, for his house was at least 10 times the size of everyone else's and it had been constructed with the finest timber.

He had acres upon acres of land and sheds which housed horses, pigs and cattle. His name was Acwel, and he went around villages and towns plundering the land, thieving from families and people wherever he went. Everybody knew him for he was truly feared. With all the wealth he amassed from a life of stealing, he ruled the entire county of Yorkshire. He led a small army of soldiers, which made it impossible for anyone to stand up to him. When he walked through the streets, people were so afraid they often ran in the opposite direction, for he took what he wanted whenever it suited him. Some villagers were so poor that they barely survived and if they were lucky enough to sell anything at the market, they had to make the money last for weeks at a time. Of all the cattle he owned, he never offered to help feed a poor family or give away any of his goats' milk.

Acwel relished his fame. He laughed when people ran away from him, but little did he know his laughing days were numbered, for he had crossed Edwin, who was fiercely courageous and brave beyond words. He was a soldier after all.

Edwin watched as Acwel and his wife walked through the front door of their enormous house. He imagined them sitting in a dining room together being served sumptuous banquets, eating all the food they could stuff into their greedy mouths. He imagined them drinking wine from endless barrels then dragging themselves off to sleep in a big bed with four posts on a soft, fluffy mattress stuffed full of feathers, as the rest of the village made do with a small bed on the floor using straw stuffed into fabric to keep themselves warm.

When the candles flickered out, it was time for Edwin to act. As Acwel and his wife slept, a soldier who guarded the house during the night sat next to the front door and fell fast asleep. Little did Acwel know that he had employed a solider who was clearly not up to the job of protecting him and his wife, for this particular soldier waited until the house was dark then fell fast asleep on the porch every single night he was supposed to keep guard. He didn't think it would do any harm, for this house belonged to Acwel and there was nobody in the whole of Yorkshire who would be stupid enough to harm him. As he snored away, Edwin crept into the house and looked around. He couldn't believe that there were so many rooms. Every room was filled with furniture. Tapestries hung from the walls and the rooms were decorated with ornaments scattered around on tables and the mantels. He felt more incensed than he had in his whole entire life.

He made his way into the bedroom and found the occupants sleeping soundly. On a small table on the far corner of the room, Edwin noticed some items. Among them was his gold coin. He peered over to the bed and watched Acwel sleep as he gently lifted the coin and clutched it tightly in his hand.

He continued watching Acwel as he walked out of the bedroom and back towards the front door. Just as he was about to open the door and walk through it, he stopped and turned around. He was starving and thought of all the food that Acwel would have in the house. Just a little bite of something was all he wanted, perhaps a cob of bread or an apple. He stepped away from the door and into the kitchen, where he saw rows of cupboards and shelves stacked full of food. Baskets on the floor contained sacks of potatoes, grains and wheat. He began rummaging around ever so quietly. He found some fruit, so he scooped up a few apples and tucked them into his trousers. A cob of bread had been left on a shelf and he picked it up and scoffed it down in one go. He could feel his belly as it began to swell, and it felt good.

When Edwin snuck towards the front door, an apple fell down his trousers and hit the wooden floor with a thud. All of a sudden, the sleeping soldier had slammed the door open and Acwel scurried out of his bed and came thumping down the hallway. Edwin pushed the soldier out of the way and ran as fast as his legs could carry him. "Get him!" yelled Acwel. The other soldiers awoke and ran after Edwin. A mighty scuffle ensued and by the time the fight was over, only one man was standing.

Acwel had dressed and waited for his soldiers to return. As he waited, he realised he was completely on his own and he felt utterly helpless, so he sat nervously in front of his fireplace, just like the coward he was. He jumped at every sound and even had his wife check outside when a cow began mooing in a nearby field. Without his soldiers, he was nothing, unprotected, and the longer he waited, he eventually realised his soldiers would not be returning to the house. He wondered how long it would take for the villagers to start turning on him.

The following morning, Acwel's soldiers had still not returned, and he knew that the person who had been in his house had won the fight. Edwin told all of the market stall owners that he retrieved his stolen coin from Acwel, something that had never been done before. Word quickly spread within the village that Acwel was without his soldiers.

By noon, all of the villagers had descended upon Acwel's house. They pounded on his door with their bare fists, for they all had something stolen by him and now they wanted it back. Acwel cowered in the corner of his living room among his lavish furnishings and grand tapestries that hung from the walls. The door came off its hinges and thudded onto the floor. The villagers pilfered through every drawer, every cupboard, every inch of space and reclaimed their belongings. They ate all his food and retrieved all of their animals. Gone were the cows, sheep, goats and chickens. The fields were empty.

After the villagers retrieved their belongings and ate like kings, Acwel was captured and walked through the streets. People cheered and waved their hands in the air. They all marched him out of Yorkshire and instructed him never to return. His wife was too ashamed to stay, so she left with him. She was never seen again.

Edwin the soldier was now a hero. He got his gold coin back and the villagers felt safe once again. Word spread throughout the land about the hero called Edwin and soon reached Ethelberht, the Anglo-Saxon king of England. He summoned Edwin to his castle on the outskirts of Kent and knighted him for his courage and bravery. Edwin was no longer a mercenary, an ordinary man, a soldier; he was now Sir Edwin, and King Ethelberht gave him a diamond as a very special gift to mark the occasion. The diamond was shaped into a triangle and Edwin wondered what to do with it. A very precious and valuable jewel had to be protected, so he decided to have the diamond set into the coin.

Sir Edwin wore the coin, with its diamond, around his neck every day, for he was very proud to be given such a special gift from the King. He lived a full and happy life and even married. When the years wore on, Sir Edwin grew old and died at the ripe old age of 50.

Because he was such a hero, it was right that he be buried in a manner befitting a hero. The helmet he wore in battle and the sword he carried with him in life was placed beside his body in a chamber on a ship. The ship then headed for his birthplace in southern Scandinavia for Sir Edwin's wife decided that he should be buried in the country where he was born. The very day after the ship set sail, a high wind gathered and the seas turned rough. A storm blew in and the sails thrashed about. The boat swayed from side to side, and it never made its journey to Scandinavia. It is unclear what happened to the sailors, and nobody ever found the ship. That is, not until many years later.

Edwin's coin was passed down to his daughter. Her name was Mildritha, and when she died, she left the coin to her son. For the next 400 years, the coin was passed down from parent to child.

CHAPTER 7

On the 5th of January 1066, Edward the Confessor died, and England's crown was passed down to Harold Godwinson. A few months later, something very strange happened. One evening, people began running out of their homes into the cold and looked above. A series of bright lights blazed across the sky. People gasped in awe as they witnessed the phenomenon that was happening above them. Children sat on their father's shoulders and marvelled at the magnificent array of light that flooded the sky.

A large meteor had exploded and as it shot through the sky, it broke up into millions of pieces. By the time the rock had hit Earth, thousands of little fragments of rock had fallen to the ground. In a small fishing village off the coast of Eastern England, the residents woke to find some of the tiny fragments scattered around the village. As they set about cleaning up the mess, a young girl called Beatrice put on her coat, grabbed a broom from the family kitchen and began sweeping the little path that led to her front door. Sweeping up the debris into a little pile, she noticed something glistening among the rubble. She bent down curiously and picked up the small stone. She brushed off the dirt with the hem of her dress and when she had finished cleaning it, a bright blue aquamarine gem sparkled. She ran to her mother and showed her the gem. When the girl's father came home from fishing, they proudly showed him the gem and they all agreed it was a gift from the heavens.

They did not know what to do with the gem and thought it would be bad luck to sell it, so they decided to have it set into the coin with the diamond that had been passed down through the generations from parent to child. They went about finding a jeweller and several weeks later were on their way to London. The jeweller set the blue aquamarine stone at the top of the diamond. The family were overjoyed, for it was breathtaking. The coin now had two stones, the crystal white diamond and the blue aquamarine gem.

Beatrice's parents died in 1098 and she did not marry or have any children. The house where she grew up became her own and she decided to spend the rest of her days living in the fishing village where she knew everyone. Beatrice was well liked by all accounts, and often took her father's boat out to sea to catch fish. One windy afternoon she sat in the little boat untangling nets. She was concentrating so much that she didn't realise the current was taking the boat further out to sea. When she finished with the nets she looked up and was so far out to sea that she couldn't even see the shores of England.

In a panic Beatrice grabbed the oars but one fell into the water. When she reached over to grab it, the oar drifted further away. With only one oar she paddled to the left of the boat then paddled to the right so she was paddling in a straight line. However, the sea's currents were too strong and after an hour Beatrice still couldn't see the shore as the current kept pulling her back. She was exhausted and had no option but to sit in the boat to gather her strength to start paddling again.

Several weeks later a seagull landed on the boat that had lain upside down drifting in the sea. Tied to the boat was a bag of rotten food that Beatrice had packed for lunch on that very fateful day she went fishing. Over the following months the bag had also loosened from the boat and eventually drifted away. And in that little bag was the coin, for Beatrice had taken it everywhere since her parents had passed away. Gone was Beatrice, perished at sea, and gone was the coin. Lost at sea, forever. So it would seem.

In the 13th century, London Bridge was a vibrant and busy place in which to trade as market stall owners came from all over London to sell their goods on the bridge. The bridge was packed with stalls and dwellings that were several storeys high. Underneath the bridge, high arches were built so that boats could easily move up and down the river. The Thames was bustling with boats and hundreds of docks scattered up and down it, which allowed merchants from England and Europe to trade everything from corn, to wool, to salt and fish.

In the year 1212, a French woman named Lucienne lived above a shop on London Bridge, where she sold bread. Every morning she woke at 5 o'clock and walked the 15-minute journey to the baker, placed her bread in a sack and tied it on her back.

As Lucienne walked back to the bridge, she said good morning to the traders whom she saw every day. It was a hot July morning and Lucienne was completely unaware that a fire had started in the London borough of Southwark, just a few hundred yards away. High winds fuelled the fire and it quickly spread to London Bridge. Cinders sparked the thatched roofs of the buildings, which caused the fire to jump to the other side of the river. Hundreds of people were trapped as both ends of the bridge were raging with fire. Everything on the bridge had been built with wood and it caused an almighty inferno. People jumped off the bridge into the water and swam to rescue boats.

People lost their worldly possessions and their livelihoods. The bridge pylons that were made of stone survived, but the damage was so great that nothing could be rebuilt on it for many years afterwards.

When the fire was eventually brought under control, all that was left was the smokey embers and charcoal debris. Volunteers began the gruelling task of cleaning up the mess. Owners who had lost their stalls stood in dismay in front of the wreckage and wondered how they would rebuild. Families who returned to their homes rummaged through the wreckage to find anything that may have survived. Lucienne stood at the bridge and began to cry for she did not have the money to rebuild. Her whole life had been swallowed up in the fire and she had no way of earning an income, no way to buy food for herself or pay rent. She looked around at the rubble one last time, turned around and walked to the edge of the riverbank. She sat down and buried her head in her hands in utter despair.

"What am I to do?" she cried. "I am done for."

Then all of a sudden, the sky began to clear. What started as a cloudy day suddenly became bright. The sun pierced through the clouds and they, too, disappeared. A deep blue colour filled the sky and Lucienne looked up to the sun. A bright sunbeam shone down, and she wondered how the weather could change so quickly after such a dull and dreary morning. She followed the sunbeam with her eyes and on the ground just under the bridge, she saw a coin. Her heart jumped. She bent over, scooped it up and there it was, glimmering in her hand. The coin with its diamond and aquamarine stone. Just like little Beatrice, she brushed off the dirt with her dress and next to the aquamarine stone was a bright orange stone of citrine. It was the colour of fire, just like the fire that had ravaged London Bridge. *Tis a miracle*, marvelled Lucienne.

"With this coin, I shall make a new life for thee," she whispered as she clutched it tightly in her hands.

And so she tucked the coin into her purse, never to return to the banks of the river or the bridge where she had sold bread every day for the past 30 years. She packed a bag, left London and travelled all the way to Kirkstall Abbey in the middle of England where she met an order of monks. They were known as the Cistercian monks and people often went to them if they wanted to sell something valuable. The monks traded anything of value for land and money and when the monks saw Lucienne's coin, they offered a handsome sum of money in exchange for it.

She gladly accepted the offer and left the abbey a wealthy woman. She soon became the owner of land and had a house built on it. She lived the rest of her life in a nice, comfortable home that was warm, and her store room was always full of fresh food.

CHAPTER 8

The coin remained within the abbey walls for the next hundred years. As the elder monks grew old and died, a new generation slowly took over. This new generation were mostly nuns. They had no idea that the coin had sat hidden in a bedroom within the abbey walls. The monk who hid the coin died suddenly and had not told anyone of the coin's whereabouts. After his burial, the bedroom was cleared of his belongings and the room sat unoccupied until one of the nuns asked if she could make it her own. It was agreed and she spent the next 10 years sleeping in a room with the coin. The nun's name was Agnes and her sister, Emma, visited every month. Sometimes they spent their time walking around the grounds of the abbey, chuckling as they told silly tales to one another. One afternoon as the women were sitting on a stone wall, Emma told Agnes she was to be married. Agnes was delighted and was eager to meet her new brother-in-law. She had heard wonderful stories about him and was happy to see her sister, whom she loved dearly, talk about him so fondly.

Two months later, Agnes met her new brother-in-law. His name was Ivo and he greeted Agnes with a warm hug. During one of their visits it started to rain, so they thought it best to stay indoors. Agnes suggested they sit in her room so they could talk and not disturb anyone. She pulled up the chair from her desk and borrowed another from the bedroom opposite hers. She poured tea and they ate bread and butter with cheese. Agnes pulled her bed a few inches away from the wall to be near to Emma and whilst doing so, Ivo noticed a little gap in the wall behind the bed. He squinted his eyes and followed the small gap across the wall. He realised the little gap was square shaped and wondered what it was. He never mentioned it to Agnes or Emma, for he thought that something might be hidden inside the stone wall.

The next time Emma visited Agnes, Ivo didn't go with her, for he told her he was ill and lay in bed resting. When Emma set off for the abbey, he hopped out of bed and got dressed. He watched her climb onto her horse and gallop away. He then saddled up his horse and slowly trotted in the same direction, ensuring that he was a good distance away so as not to be seen by her. When he arrived at the abbey, he tied his horse to a nearby tree and quietly snuck inside. He knew the sisters would be walking around the gardens, so he made his way into Agnes's bedroom. He pulled the bed away from the wall, picked up his chisel and began chipping away at the stone. A few minutes later, he removed a large stone from the wall and peered inside. It was dark, and he couldn't see anything, so he put his hand in the hole and found a little wooden box. He shook the crumbling stone off the box and opened it. Wrapped in cloth, he found the coin that had lain within the walls of the abbey for over a hundred years.

When Agnes returned to her bedroom, her bed was back against the wall, and she was none the wiser. However, when Emma returned home, Ivo was gone. The next day, he stood on the eastern shores of England and waited. When the boat docked onto the shores, Ivo boarded and sailed to France. He had planned to have the diamonds and gemstones removed from the coin and sell them separately. He tried pulling the diamond out first, but it wouldn't budge. He thought the gems might be easier to remove as they were smaller, so he tried picking at them with a small knife. But alas, they wouldn't budge either. He tried twisting the tip of the knife under the gems, but they still stuck. As he sat on the boat, he scratched his head, wondering how on earth the gems and diamonds got there in the first place. And that was just it, the Earth's elements were so strong and powerful that nobody would ever be able to separate them. No force on Earth could separate the special gems. Ivo's plan had backfired, but it wasn't a total waste because he still had the coin. He just had to sell it in one piece, which would mean he wouldn't get as much for it.

Ivo soon arrived in Sangatte, on the northern coast of France. He had always wanted to travel to Europe for he thought it was a continent so big that there would be boundless opportunities for him. Little did Ivo know that a deadly disease was spreading through Europe. It was a disease that spread very quickly and would end up wiping out a third of Europe. The bubonic plague began in China and spread to Africa then quickly reached Europe. Ivo had walked straight into his own death. Within three days of arriving in France, he, too, had caught the disease. When the pus-filled boils began appearing on his neck, he thought nothing of it. However, within hours the vomiting began, then the fever, aches and chills. His whole body was in excruciating pain, and he collapsed in the small village of Calais and died. Later that night, a dozen men wearing masks with long beaks collected the dead and buried them. One such man was known as a 'plague-doctor'. When he saw Ivo lying in the street, he realised that this was not a peasant, for he wore shoes made from cowhide and his clothing looked new. He thought that Ivo must have been an important man, so he arranged for a proper Christian burial. As the undertakers placed Ivo into the burial box, they removed his shoes. The coin fell out of his shoe and rolled around onto the floor until it stopped when it collided with a wall.

Two of the undertakers looked down at the coin, then at each other. In an instant, they both dived down for the coin and were scrambling over each other on the floor to grab it. One of the men pulled the other off him and threw his arm down right onto the coin. The other man jumped up and grabbed his hand, prying his fingers away from his tight grip. His arm was bitten, and blood was drawn. He screamed in pain and let go. The man who had bitten him quickly got to his feet and bolted. A chase ensued and the two men ran as fast as they could. They ran to the beach and into the sea. Their greed had got the better of them for neither man made it back to the shore. They both drowned and as their bodies lay spread over the rippling sea, the coin washed up onto the beach with the current. The coin, with its diamond and two stones of aquamarine and citrine, glistened under the sun.

As the plague took hold, thousands of families tried to flee Europe, at least the families who could afford to. Once such family was Francis, his wife Isadora and their young daughters. They boarded a boat from Calais and Francis felt lucky to escape the Black Death. In 1348, the plague had made its way from Europe to England and as the boat pulled out of Calais, Francis saw the coin as it lay on the water's edge, shining in the sunlight. He yelled out for the boat to stop, and he jumped overboard and swam over to it. When he hopped back onto the boat, he showed his wife what he had found. When Francis and his family arrived in England, he learned that the plague was raging its way through London so they headed straight for the countryside.

Early one morning, Francis began to feel terribly unwell. Big bulges began appearing on his neck, so he wrote a letter to his sleeping wife and crept away from their campsite. After walking for a whole day, as far away from his family as he could, he sat down by a stream and rested. Wearily, he scooped up the water and drank it. He then sat down, propping himself up against a tree. He closed his eyes and sadly, he never woke up. He died happy knowing that his wife and children now had the coin and, if need be, they could sell it and live comfortably. But it was not to be, for the family had no idea what was to come. When Isadora woke and found her husband gone, she picked up the note next to where she slept and read it. She looked over at her sleeping girls and cried.

Her daughter woke and asked, "Mama, why do you cry?"

Isadora pulled her daughter close and explained that her father had caught the sickness that had taken so many lives and he had to leave so his family could live. She packed the campsite and, with her daughters, rode to a nearby village where they settled. Isadora found a job spinning wool and as her daughters grew into young ladies, they too worked, affording the family a comfortable life. They wanted for nothing and lived in a small but comfortable house.

One day in January 1362, a huge gale from the Atlantic swept through Europe and across the shores to Britain. The ferocious winds tore down houses in Ireland and by the time it reached the North Sea, it had caused a catastrophic storm. The storm wiped out villages and homes and Isadora's house was swept away along with all of the family's belongings. Isadora and her daughters scurried among the floating planks of wood looking for the coin, but it had washed away For the next 158 years, it lay at the bottom of a river, trapped under a rock. Over the years, the winter months were freezing, and one particular year, the river completely froze over.

The following spring, the ice began to break and on a warm sunny day in the year 1520, a woman named Sarah was walking alongside a river and sat down on a rock to rest. As Sarah looked down at her reflection in the shimmering water, protruding from a rock in the riverbed was a bright shiny object. She tried to grab it, but her arm wasn't long enough, so she jumped into the river and pulled at it. As she tried to pull herself out of the river, her wet clothes and the weight of her shoes dragged her down and she cried out for help. A hunter was walking in the woods and heard her cries. He ran to the river and pulled her out and they both flopped themselves onto the bank of the river. Sarah opened her hand and saw the most exquisite coin she had ever seen. She tucked it in her shoe and thanked the hunter for helping her out of the water. Then, she headed back to her village and home to her small hut where she changed into dry clothes. She had just made it, for a storm was brewing, and as the clouds turned grey, the rain began to fall. She heard a knock on the door and when she opened it, standing on the porch was the hunter. He said nothing, which made her feel quite frightened. She realised he had followed her home and knew it was because of the coin. He held out his hand.

"The coin," he demanded. "Give it."

"I'll not!" she cried.

Sarah tried to slam the door shut, but the hunter had positioned his foot over the threshold so the door wouldn't close. She pushed the door with all her strength, but the hunter was a tall man who was very strong. He pushed the door open, and she fell backwards.

"Tis mine!" she exclaimed as she got up and ran towards the back of the hut. He moved forward and as he tried to grab her, she ducked under his legs and ran out of the front door. The storm was brutal, and cattle, sheep and horses in nearby fields huddled under trees for shelter. Thunder cracked loudly and when the lightning came, the hunter saw a flash of Sarah running towards the forest. He gave chase and quickly caught up. He grabbed hold of her arm and she fell down. She lay on her stomach, clutching her coin tightly in her hand. He pulled her arm out and tried to pry her fingers open. She kicked and thrashed at him and at the exact moment when the hunter pried her fingers open and grabbed the coin, a flash of lightning flew down to Earth and hit him. An electric shock reverberated into the body of the hunter as he held the coin.

Then all of a sudden, the rain stopped and the skies cleared. When Sarah sat up and looked around, she noticed that the hunter had died of an electric shock. She looked down at him as he lay on the wet grass with his arms outstretched. His hands were open and in the palm of his left hand was the coin. She went through his pockets looking for money. She didn't find any, but what she did find was a small green stone called a peridot. She had no clue why the hunter had the stone in his pocket, but she took it anyway. The hunter had purchased the stone the previous day. He had planned to give the stone to his wife as a gift to celebrate the birth of their first child and, when they died, it was to be passed down to their daughter, but it was not to be. Sarah took the coin from the dead hunter's hand and picked it up. The lightning bolt had made a small hole in the coin, so she placed the stone of peridot into the hole so she wouldn't lose it. The something magical happened. The coin began glowing and fused the peridot into the coin where it stayed, never to be removed.

The golden amulet now had three small stones of peridot, citrine and aquamarine with a diamond in the centre. An ordinary coin from the year 600 AD, combined with the Earth's elements, had become a magical phenomenon. The diamond was the symbol of courage, the green peridot the symbol of air, the orange citrine the symbol of fire and the blue aquamarine the symbol of water. Unbeknownst to Sarah, she was now the holder of a very powerful amulet. Sarah held onto the amulet until her death in 1530. She had become very ill in the weeks leading up to her death, and on the day she died, she summoned her only child, a daughter, to her bedside.

"Take thee," Sarah raised her weak and frail hands and clutched her daughter's. She carefully placed the amulet in the palm of her daughter's hand. As soon as the amulet was handed over, Sarah died. Her daughter sobbed over the death of her beloved mother, and she placed the amulet in her pocket, not realising the journey it had been on over the past thousand years or the significance it would play in years to come. Sarah's daughter was named Adeline, and in the year 1533, on the same day Queen Elizabeth I was born, she gave birth to twin girls, who she named Elinor and Gudrun.

CHAPTER 9

Now that Jess was in on their secret, she pestered Isabel and William night and day to take her with them on their next time travelling adventure. She thought it was going to be a wonderful trip filled with excitement, but she was sorely mistaken and had no idea how dangerous each journey really was. William, being the eldest, insisted that she stay but agreed that she could come and say goodbye to Isabel on the morning of their trip. Jess woke very early and arrived at Isabel's at 8 o'clock in the morning. She sauntered through the front door and into the kitchen where a shocked Isabel and William sat eating breakfast. It was probably the only time Isabel had seen Jess dressed and at her house so early in the morning.

"Right then," said William. "Shall we go?"

"Oh Izzy." Jess threw her arms around Isabel. "I wish I were going with you. Please let me go with you."

William raised an eyebrow at Jess.

"I know," she quipped. "I can't go, but please come back safely. I couldn't bear life without you."

"We will," replied Isabel. "I promise we'll see you soon."

The children hugged their mother and headed for the door. Then a big *bang!* sound came from the kitchen. They rushed in to find Mother on the floor.

"Mum! What happened?" cried Isabel.

"Are you alright?" asked William as he helped her up and onto a chair.

"I just slipped over," replied Mother. "I've only banged my head. It's nothing."

William swept Mother's hair from her face and saw the blood trickling down her cheek. She had quite a big gash and it was already swelling up. Jess grabbed a tea towel and handed it to William, who placed it gently over the wound.

"I'm afraid you'll need stitches, Mum."

At the hospital William found a chair for his Mother in the waiting room and gently sat her down. After completing all of the registration forms, the Pritchard's were ushered into a small room and a doctor closed the curtain around the bed. "I'm Doctor Jones, but you can call me Matt." The doctor looked very young and William thought he probably graduated from medical school quite recently. He would loved to have chatted about the medical profession and his university studies but now wasn't the time. "I'm Will, and this is my mum, Elinor."

After observing the nasty cut on Mother's head Doctor Jones informed William that stitches and an overnight stay under observation was required, for the fall had caused a severe concussion. William knew exactly what this meant. He would have to stay behind and take care of Mother. He felt quite anxious about going through the trees anyway, for her state of mind was fragile and he wondered whether she could really look after herself if she was on her own.

"Izzy, I can't go with you," he said solemnly.

"Oh no!" she cried. "I need you, but I know that Mum needs you too."

"We can't put it off until Mum is better. The bump on her head will heal, but I just don't think she should be left alone, especially when we don't know when we'll be home."

"What are we going to do?" cried Isabel.

Jess jumped out of her seat in the waiting room. "I'll go!" she shouted.

Isabel and William got such a fright they just almost jumped out of their skin.

"No, really! I'll go with you."

"What if something happens to you?" asked William. "I can't guarantee you'll be safe."

"I've done it before," she replied. "And yes, I know it was only a couple of hours, but Izzy spent weeks in 1851 and she made it back. We'll be able to protect each other and look out for one another."

William realised it wasn't such a bad idea. He knew that Isabel would struggle to look after their mother on her own and Jess did have a good argument. And so it was settled.

Later that day the girls walked from Isabel's home in Richmond back to Kew Gardens. They were lucky that there were enough trees in Kew Gardens that were planted in so many different centuries. It meant they didn't have to walk very far to get back to their tree. When they arrived at Kew Gardens, Jess was very excited. Thanks to William's careful planning, they did not go to the first tree they travelled through, for that would have taken them back to 1748.

William thought it would be best if they returned the amulet when King George III was on the throne, for it matched the timing of him wearing the amulet in the painting. Isabel and Jess walked past the tree that took them to 1748 and over to a similar sized tree in another area of the gardens. Together, they slapped their hands on the tree and closed their eyes. Sure enough, they had arrived in 1768 to return the amulet to King George III.

When Isabel began walking away from the tree, she almost fell over, for her feet became stuck under the numerous layers of petticoats under her dress. She pulled her dress up above her dainty shoes and admired her turquoise blue frock. She imagined William standing next to her with a silk coat, frilly shirt and knickerbockers and tights. How she would have laughed. She missed him already.

They had reached their destination, for they had arrived at the big red house they now knew as Kew Palace.

While the house itself looked beautiful among the magnificent gardens, something didn't feel right to Isabel. She had a strange feeling that they were being watched. Jess sensed her uneasiness.

"Are you okay?" asked Jess.

"I'm just not sure about this."

"What do you mean?"

"Well," said Isabel. "For a couple of months, I've felt as though someone has been watching me. Sometimes when I walk home from school, I feel as though someone is following me. I'm having that same feeling now."

Jess looked around. "There's no one here but us. Don't worry about it, we're in this together."

When the girls walked up the stairs to the front door, Isabel wasn't exactly sure what to do without

William, but she knew she had to return the amulet to the King.

"What do we do with the amulet?" whispered Jess.

"William said we had to get it to the King somehow," replied Isabel. "We can't just leave it at the front door. We need to go inside. Maybe someone can pass it on to him."

"Are you kidding? Last time we got chased out by a man and I ended up going through that magic tree."

Isabel squeezed Jess's hand. "I understand if you're scared, I am too, but we'll just sneak in and out and hopefully nobody will notice. We're dressed like everyone else here, so we won't look out of place."

"I guess you're right."

Isabel clutched the big brass doorknob and tried turning it. "It's locked," she whispered. "Let's go round the back."

The girls crept quietly around the side of the building until they reached the back of the house. Perfectly manicured lawns and shrubs decorated the lovely garden. Beds of red roses and blue geraniums lined a path that led to a pagoda where a burst of purple wisteria dangled from the wooden rafters.

"It's beautiful," whispered Jess.

Apart from the front doors, two heavy-set doors at the back of the house was the only other entrance that they could see. Isabel twisted the knob. It was locked. "I guess we'll have to wait until someone comes out." By the time Isabel had finished her sentence, Jess was already climbing into a nearby window. Fumbling around in her big frilly dress with its endless petticoats and frills, she thrust her leg over and stumbled onto the floor inside. A few seconds later, she popped her head out the window and waved at Isabel.

"Well done!" Isabel was very impressed.

The girls found themselves in a very simple-looking room with a fireplace and a small bed. There were no carpets or rugs on the floor, just bare wood, where a tiny mouse scurried in a hole under a floorboard. There weren't any tapestries or paintings on the walls as one might expect to find in a palace. In the corner of the room, a jug of water sat on a wooden table. Isabel realised she was in one of the servant's rooms.

"Over here," said Jess. She opened the door and a long corridor led to the kitchen. The girls tip-toed to the side of the kitchen and watched as half a dozen servants scurried around with silver trays while kitchen staff placed dainty little plates of meat garnished with vegetables and herbs onto trays. Cooks stirred broths and stews in enormous pots over open fires. The kitchen was warm and smelled delicious; however, the girls knew that they couldn't be seen, so they turned around and soon found themselves in the library. They recognised it immediately, for it was the very room where they were chased out by the man in 2014.

There was nobody in the library, so the girls stepped inside. On one side of the room, the walls were filled with paintings. Several were a young King George III, one dressed in a red velvet jacket with a blue sash over it, while other paintings were with his family, Queen Charlotte and their children standing alongside them. However, the painting that the girls had seen was nowhere in sight, for it hadn't been painted yet.

Along the other side of the walls sat rows of books gathering dust. Isabel began at one end and Jess at the other. Together they gazed at all the spines. There were hundreds of books from Shakespeare's sonnets to his plays, such as *Macbeth*, *Hamlet* and *A Midsummer Night's Dream*. Isabel pulled a very old-looking book from a shelf and read the cover, *The Odyssey* by Homer. She was familiar with Homer as William had studied *The Odyssey* last year and was fascinated that it took 10 years for its protagonist, Odysseus, to return home from the Trojan War. Isabel remembered a discussion William had with Mother about it, and at the time, Isabel thought that Odysseus was pretty stupid if it took 10 years when all he had to do was hop on a boat and sail home. William had rolled his eyes at Isabel's naivety and told her that it was what he did over the 10 years that made the book so interesting. Isabel turned to Jess. "I hope we get home quicker than Odysseus!"

Jess pulled out a book that looked new. She opened the leather cover and inside it read 'A Dictionary of the English Language by Samuel Johnson'. Unbeknownst to Jess, she was holding a copy of England's first English dictionary. She flipped open the pages and began reading.

"Ha ha! Look at this, Izzy. The definition of *Lunch* is ‹as much food as one's hand can hold'."

"That's hilarious," replied Isabel. "Here's another one. *Fart*: 'wind from behind'." The girls burst out laughing then Isabel realised they were making too much noise. "Shhhhh!" She nudged Jess. "Pretty funny though."

Jess carefully placed the dictionary back on the shelf.

"Alright," said Isabel. "I suppose we leave the amulet on the desk. We can't just walk through the palace and ask for the King. I know William said that's what we had to do, but I just can't do it. I'm too scared."

Isabel studied the amulet properly for the first time. Its diamond and three small stones of aquamarine, citrine and peridot looked stunning. She wondered how such a small object could be so powerful as to yield immortality. Wondering where to leave the amulet, she sat on the big leather chair behind the desk. Six drawers on either side of the desk were tightly shut, but curiosity got the better of her. She knew that what was inside the drawers was none of her business, but she just couldn't help herself. Instinctively, she looked around to see if anybody was watching, although she and Jess were the only people in the room, apart from all the faces in the paintings staring back down at her. She carefully pulled the top drawer open. *How dull*, she thought, for all the drawer contained was paper and bottles of black ink.

"What are you doing?" asked Jess as she watched Isabel rummaging through the desk. "We shouldn't be going through this stuff. It's not ours." As Jess walked over to the desk, she, too, couldn't help herself and she bent down and opened the bottom drawers. Again, more papers and writing quills lay neatly in the drawers. Just then the girls heard footsteps. They quickly shut the drawers and hid under the desk. The door opened and a young boy entered the room. He scurried behind a plant stand and crouched down. A few moments later, another young boy ran in. "I'm looking for you," he said in a soft voice. The little boy behind the plant stand began giggling.

"Ha! There you are!" The boys chuckled and darted out of the room together. The little princes were Frederick and William, second and third sons of King George III. When the girls thought it was safe, they climbed out from under the desk.

"Let's get out of here," whispered Jess. "This place scares me."

"Agreed," replied Isabel. "We've returned the amulet, now it's time to go home."

Just as the girls headed towards the door, it burst open once again and in ran the two princes. The girls and the princes stood facing each other, not knowing what to say or do. Isabel placed her finger over her mouth.

"Ssshhhhh," she whispered. "Don't tell anyone."

And just then, little Frederick gave an almighty scream. "Mama! Mama!"

The girls bolted and ran through the corridor. At the end of the corridor, servants ran towards the girls who turned around and ran towards the front door. Jess tugged on the big handle, but it was locked. She ran towards the stairs, grabbing Isabel on the way, and they fled up the staircase. They ran into a room where a big grand bed sat against the wall. Three gentlemen in the room all stopped and stared straight at the girls. Two of the men were attending to a man who was standing on a stool. They had pins embedded in pin cushions that were tied to their wrists. Tape measures hung from around their necks. They looked absolutely horrified when they saw the girls barge in. They looked up at the man and waited for him to say something. He waved his hand, and they gracefully bowed their heads and quietly left the room. The man stepped off the stool and scratched his scalp under the big white wig that sat neatly on his head.

"Do you know who I am?" he bellowed.

"No, sir," replied an utterly frightened Isabel.

"You mean to tell me that you don't know who I am?" he said.

"No, sir," repeated Isabel.

"But you look very important," cried Jess.

"That's because I *am* very important."

It dawned on Isabel that she was standing right in front of King George III and was about to get a right royal telling off from him.

"I am King George III, King of England, and you have no right to be in my private rooms."

Looking down at the girls, who were white with fear, he realised that they were just as shocked as he. "Well then," he said. "Who are you and from where do you hail?"

"I... um... I'm Isabel Pritchard and this is Jess Green."

"We're best friends," quipped Jess.

Isabel gave Jess a nudge. "Shhhh," she whispered. "And, um... we live in London."

"Ahhhh, London," said the King. It seemed as though the mention of the word *London* put the King at ease, for he sat on a nearby chair and looked out of the big windows that overlooked the gardens.

"I recently acquired a new home in London for my family and my beloved queen. We call it *The Queen's House*." His relaxed disposition now turned to a stern frown. "You haven't told me why you are trespassing on sovereign land."

"We are here to give you this." Isabel opened her hand and the amulet sparkled. The King's eyes popped when he saw it. He picked it up and marvelled at the spectacular diamond and gems.

"It's splendid," he gushed. "Where did you find it?"

"Well," said Isabel. "I've had it for a long time and my family felt that it needs to be kept with all the Crown's jewels."

"And that is the reason you are here?"

"Yes," replied Isabel.

The King rubbed his chin. "You look rather familiar. Is it possible that we have met before?"

Isabel felt a very uneasy feeling come over her. "I don't think so," she said nervously.

"The more I think of it, the more I am certain of it," he said as he stood up and began pacing.

"That's it! You look just like the girl who saved me from drowning when I was a young boy. As a matter of fact," he went on, "you look identical."

Isabel realised the King had remembered her when she travelled to 1748. He was 10 years old, and after all these years, he still remembered that she had saved his life. However good his memory was, Isabel was now in real trouble, for while the King had grown from that little boy and was now 30 years old, she was still the same 13-year-old girl. How would she explain this? Worse still, she had to explain this to *the King*! The one person who held so much power that all he had to do was snap his fingers and a dozen guards could take her and lock her away.

The panic set in and Isabel wondered whether she should just grab Jess and run, but then she realised he had guards everywhere, and ones with horses! They wouldn't get far at all, not far enough to outrun the horses to the tree where they could get back home. *Oh no! What do I do?* she thought.

The King bent down to Isabel and looked deep into her eyes.

"You are her daughter," he said quietly. "It is you, is it not?"

"Yes!" she replied. "It was my mother who saved you from drowning. She told me about it."

"Where is she now?" he asked.

"Oh, she's very ill."

"Close to death," quipped Jess.

"That is indeed very unfortunate," said the King. He looked rather despondent at hearing the news. "Well then, young ladies, I thank you for this exquisite gift, and Isabel, I cannot express enough my gratitude to your mother for saving my life. I am indeed saddened to hear she is poorly. Are you hungry?"

The girls looked at each other.

"We need to get back home," said Isabel.

"Oh, but you must eat," said the King.

"We really must go. Our brother is waiting for us."

"Well, alright then. If you must go."

The King's butler ushered the girls down the stairs just as a maid was wheeling a trolley towards the sitting room. The girls stood in utter amazement at the sight. On the trolley sat half a dozen cakes. Chocolate ripple, sponges with jam and cream, fruit cakes with glazed strawberries on top.

"I guess we could stay for tea," whispered Jess.

"Mmmmm, they look so good," said Isabel.

"I'm soooooo hungry."

The maid stopped the trolley. "Will yers be stayin' for tea?"

"Yes, please!" said the girls excitedly.

"Well then, make yerselves at home in the sitting room and I'll make an extra pot."

The girls stepped into the same room where Isabel had chatted with the young Prince George after saving him from drowning. Everything was exactly the same, so they made themselves comfortable on the sofa near a table that was laid out with dainty cups and saucers and a freshly brewed pot of tea. Young Frederick and William bounded in, pushing past each other, and sat opposite Isabel and Jess. As soon as they noticed they had company, all of a sudden, the excitable boys sat in stony silence. They hadn't had company for tea before and didn't know what to make of it.

Jess thought she may as well say something. "Hello again."

The boys looked at each other and giggled.

"What are your names?" she asked. "I'm Jess and this is my best friend, Isabel."

"I'm Frederick and *his* name is wee-wee pants," said Frederick, pointing to his little brother.

"Tis not!" replied the younger boy, folding his arms in a huff.

Isabel sat next to him and gave him a little cuddle. "Of course it's not," she said. "That's just silly. Tell me then, what's your name?"

"William."

"That's a lovely name. My brother is also called William."

"Where is he?"

"Oh, he's at home with my mother."

"My mother is a queen," said Frederick. "And my older brother George will be king one day. But he's only six. I'm five, and wee-wee pants, I mean William, is almost four."

"Do you mind if we stay for tea?" asked Isabel. "Those cakes look delicious."

"You may stay," replied Frederick.

The door opened and a different maid wheeled in the trolley of cakes. Oh my, how lovely they looked. More cakes had been added to the trolley. There were slices of apple cake, warm scones with jam and cream in little ceramic jars and sponge cakes with lemon icing. The girls were starving and drooled over the cakes as they were being cut. The maid served tea and the children ate in silence.

CHAPTER 10

When the little princes finished their cake, a nanny cleaned up the crumbs on the floor and ushered them towards the door. As the boys bounced out of the drawing room, they almost knocked over the King and his guest, who were entering the room.

The King did not look pleased, for he gave the nanny a stern look of disapproval and apologised to his guest. When the girls noticed the King was in the room, they quickly stood up, Jess curtseying and Isabel bowing as crumbs fell from her dress. The King thought this was rather amusing and motioned for them to sit down. He joined the girls on the sofa and introduced his guest, Mr Joseph Banks.

He told the girls that Mr Banks was a scientist and botanist and, with his friend James Cook, was planning a voyage to the South Pacific. Mr Banks talked about their ship, the *Endeavour*, and how they were going to sail around the world. Isabel had heard of Joseph Banks at the excursion to Kew Gardens and was quite taken by him. She loved the way he was so passionate about his upcoming expedition.

Isabel recalled Mrs Struber telling the class about Mr Banks's successful trip whereby he would return after a long voyage with over a thousand species of plants and seeds that were previously unknown to Britain. He would become instrumental in the creation of Kew Gardens. He and King George III had become very good friends over their passion for botany, and because of this, the King earned the nickname 'Farmer George'. Of course, he didn't mind, for he was gentle and kind and a loving family man.

By the time tea was finished, the girls had eaten several slices of cake each. They politely asked the King if they could go home. He wished them well, and when Isabel stood up, she felt very giddy on her feet. She swayed a little then everything around her seemed to go blurry. She tried to take a step but stumbled and fell, fainting on King George's hundred-year-old Persian rug. The King jumped up and summoned a servant who was waiting outside the door while Mr Banks scooped up Isabel's head and patted her cheeks.

When Isabel woke, she was lying in a big bed with four posts and Jess by her side. She felt awfully unwell and couldn't even lift her head from the pillow.

"What happened?" she whispered.

"You fainted," replied Jess. "When you came around, you complained of having pains in your tummy."

"I can still feel them."

"Do you think we ate too much cake?" asked Jess.

"Not me. I've eaten way more than that. It must have been something in the cake. My stomach really hurts. What about you?"

"I'm fine and I ate way more cake than you."

"We really need to get home," said a worried Isabel. "But I don't think I can get up."

"Don't worry, the King said we can stay here until you are better."

"What a nice man." Isabel closed her eyes and fell back to sleep.

Jess thought it best to let Isabel rest, so she gently pulled the blankets up to Isabel's neck and quietly left the room. She walked down the stairs and along the corridor towards the kitchen. The maid who had served tea and cake suddenly appeared. She gave Jess a warm smile and asked her if she would like to have something to eat.

"Oh no, thank you. I'm quite full from all the cake."

The maid took Jess by the hand.

"I'm Edina. Come, I'll show you around the palace."

Jess thought Edina was lovely to take such a keen interest in her. They began on the ground floor, walking through the main hall. The dark wood panelling on the walls made the hallway look drab and gloomy. With no carpet, their footsteps echoed and sounded rather eerie. They made their way into the King's dining room where a large marble fireplace kept the room warm in the evenings. In the middle of the room sat a large rectangular table with a white tablecloth on top. Only two chairs were positioned around the table and Jess assumed the King liked to dine with Queen Charlotte alone. Perhaps they needed the privacy to discuss important matters to do with the monarchy, or maybe they simply adored each other and loved to be in each other's company, away from the noisy children. The walls were decorated in a light green while several mirrors on the walls had beautifully decorated gold borders. On the far side of the room, a tall rectangular box sat next to a window. It had 50 brass pipes running from the top down to a keyboard. It looked magnificent. Jess walked over to it and pressed a key.

"Tis the King's fav'rite," said Edina.

"What's it called?" asked Jess.

"It's a chamber organ."

"Does the King play?"

"Oh goodness no." Edina chuckled. "Someone comes to play for him. His favourite composer is Handel."

"I can play too. I'm quite good actually."

"Oh my! Your family must be very substantial."

Jess wasn't quite sure what Edina meant. "Substantial? Oh, right. We're not rich, but my parents can afford lessons."

"Well then, you must play the chamber organ one day. I would love to hear you play."

"That would be lovely." Jess wondered how different the chamber organ would sound compared to her piano at home. *I'd love to have a go and see what it sounds like.*

They walked through the kitchen where a dozen servants and cooks scurried around. In the middle of the kitchen sat a huge wooden table built from an elm tree. Small rooms off the kitchen had specialised functions. The wet larder stored meat and fish, a bakehouse for bread and a scullery for cleaning the enormous amount of dishes after each meal. On the other side of the kitchen, a door led to a courtyard with a well. Fresh vegetables were also grown in the gardens.

The girls walked up the stairs and stopped at the door of the Queen's boudoir. Edina put her ear to the door and, when she heard nothing, carefully opened it.

"We can't go in," she whispered. "'Tis the Queen's rooms and nobody is allowed without permission."

It didn't matter as Jess was able to take a good look at the room from the doorway. There were chaise lounges and dainty little chairs scattered around a fireplace. The Queen often sat with her female companions and spent hours doing 'women's work', a name in the Georgian era for needlework, knotting and spinning, as they gossiped about the goings-on in Georgian society. Gold curtains hung from the windows, as well as several chairs and a table with a deck of cards that sat neatly on top of the table.

The second floor consisted mainly of bedrooms and bathrooms. The King had five children so far. George, Frederick, William, Charlotte and Edward and the three elder children shared a bedroom while the babies, Charlotte and Edward, shared a nursery.

"Well, that's all I can show," said Edina. "What did you think?"

"I loved it!" replied Jess. "I can't believe I'm in a *real* palace, with *real* kings and queens."

Edina chuckled as they walked back down the stairs. "There you go now. Back to your friend's bedroom."

Edina continued walking down the corridor and left Jess to check on Isabel. When Jess walked towards the bedroom, she was met by a man who stepped right in front of her and blocked her way. He was about 50 years of age, quite tall, and when he looked down at Jess, he looked rather intimidating. With his hands behind his back, he glared right down at Jess, who felt utterly petrified.

"Excuse me," she said, taking a sidewards step. The man also stepped sidewards so she couldn't pass.

"Do you know who I am?" he spoke in a deep voice.

"No, sir."

"I am Bartholomew Dankworth, Groom of the Bedchamber – the King's first servant. I have been his most trusted employee since he was a very young prince."

"That's nice," replied Jess as she tried looking down the hallway to see if anyone was around.

"And I know what you and that girl are," he growled.

"You're making me feel scared," said Jess. "Have we done something to upset you?"

"Yes! You and that witch."

"Witch? What do you mean?"

The man bent down until he was eye to eye with Jess.

"Twenty years ago, a little girl saved King George from drowning. He was 10 years old, and she was only a few years older, at most. Twenty years later, the King is now 30 and that same girl is back in this house and she has not aged!"

"Err... no, sir, it isn't true."

"Do not disagree! I know it is her. I am going to have you imprisoned. I know you are witches!"

The man grabbed Jess's arm and began dragging her away from the bedroom where Isabel was sleeping and towards the staircase. Jess screamed "Let me go!" She tugged at his arm and tried to pull hers away to break free, but it was no use. Mr Dankworth was very tall and very strong.

"Below stairs!" he bellowed. "Take her away!"

It wasn't long before all of the maids, servants and cooks had stopped what they were doing and scurried towards the commotion.

"Mr Dankworth! What is the purpose of this?" said a cook who had emerged from the kitchen with a dishcloth over her shoulder and her hands on her hips.

"Witches!" the man shouted.

The staff all gasped in horror, then the whispers followed.

"It's not true!" cried Jess. "Please believe me."

"Wake the sleeping girl," came a voice.

"Ask the sleeping girl, is it true?" came another.

It appeared that the whole house was ganging up on Jess, for they looked very annoyed. Mr Dankworth marched Jess into a small dark room off the kitchen and bolted the door shut.

"We must inform the King," said the cook as she followed him back into the kitchen.

"We'll do no such thing," he snapped. "We shall not bother him with this. Why, he has more important matters to deal with." Mr Dankworth turned towards the kitchen staff. "Anyone who opens this door shall be dismissed of their duties with immediate effect."

The staff quickly returned to their duties, muttering all sorts of things under their breaths. Nobody dared open the door, for Mr Dankworth was someone not to be reckoned with. As the King's main servant, he held a substantial amount of influence in the palace and could easily sway the King's decision to his own advantages.

Jess stood behind the door, wondering what to do. A small window let a little light into the room and it was getting dark. She looked around the small store room where baskets were stacked on top of one another on one side, and at the other side, sat a small table with some odd-looking kitchen utensils. Jess pulled the table over to the window, levelled it right underneath and climbed up until her chin was aligned with the bottom of the window. Not quite tall enough to pull herself up and climb through, she plonked herself down on the table and waited.

Jess wondered what would happen to Isabel. What did they do to witches in the 18th century? She had no clue and quite frankly didn't want to wait around to find out, for there had to be a way of escaping. But how? *That's it!* She tugged at the baskets, and they toppled down to the floor. Turning each one upside down Jess placed several of them on top of the table and carefully climbed up onto the baskets, squeezing herself out of the small window. When her legs were out, Jess ran from the palace towards the tree.

Upon reaching the tree, she stopped just before placing her hands upon it. One option would be to go home and bring back William, who would be able to help Isabel get home, or stay and do her best to get Isabel out of the palace. Jess knew it was dangerous going back to the palace. What if someone saw her? She just couldn't get caught again. And what if she couldn't wake Isabel? What if Isabel was too ill to get out of bed and make her way back to the tree?

Jess turned around and headed back towards the palace. There was no way she could leave Isabel there on her own. Isabel needed her more than ever and she just couldn't leave without her. Sneaking back in and not getting caught was her only option.

Back at the palace, Jess very slowly turned the big brass handle and opened the door ever so slightly. The butler, who usually opened the front door to guests, was in the library, for Jess could see him winding up the big grandfather clock. She darted up the stairs and ran to Isabel's bedroom, burst open the door, and to her shock, Isabel was gone.

The bed covers had been pulled back and Jess wondered whether Isabel had simply woken up and gone looking for her or whether that mean Mr Dankworth had taken her. Jess knew that if she ran around the palace looking for Isabel, she would be caught and returned to the store room. There was only one option left.

Jess had to bring William back to help so she ran back to the tree and placed her hands upon it. Closing her eyes, the dizziness overwhelmed her and she felt sick to her stomach. When she opened her eyes, she was desperate to know if she had travelled home to 2014 or if she was still in 1768. Running through the gardens she saw the huge glasshouse and felt relieved knowing that it hadn't been built until the 1800s. Exactly what year she wasn't sure, but it didn't matter for she was almost home. And so was the other person who had also travelled through the trees with her.

CHAPTER 11

Jess ran through the gardens and, in the distance, heard the screeching of cars and buses. She was thankful that Isabel's house was walking distance because she had no idea how she would get to there without any money. Arriving at the exit, she jogged along the main road then realised another pair of feet were running behind her. She stopped and looked around and got the shock of her life. Standing right behind her was Edina, the servant who had shown her around the palace.

"What are *you* doing here?" she asked.

"I'm sorry, Miss," replied Edina. "I saw you looking for your friend and wanted to help you find her. I followed you and when you touched that tree, I touched it too, from the other side. I don't know why you did that, and I wanted to find out why."

Looking around, Edina noticed the cars and buses zooming along the busy roads. She was horrified. "Where are we? What is all the noise and what are those on the path?" Edina stepped back against the wall of Kew Gardens and began to cry. "What is happening?"

Jess took her hand. "It's okay, you won't understand until I fully explain, but you are in the future."

The colour drained from Edina's face and she looked as though she were about to faint.

"That tree you touched is magic," said Jess. "I don't understand it either, but the girl I've been looking for, well, her name is Isabel, and her family can travel through trees. It's a special kind of magic within their family and it goes back hundreds of years."

"How do I return home?" cried Edina.

"You *will* and you *can* return home," assured Jess. "I can help you, but I need to find Isabel's brother, who can help us both. Are you ready to trust me?"

"I trust you," replied Edina.

Jess and Edina ran all the way back to Isabel's house. When they arrived, they explained everything to William. He was quite shocked to see someone from the past arrive into his own time. Before he could get his head around the whole saga, he had to put that aside, for he needed to go back to 1768 and find Isabel. He kissed his mother goodbye and said he would be back very soon. Since Isabel had left with the amulet, Mother's health had improved already. William felt confident that she would be alright on her own for a few hours.

On the way back to Kew Gardens, however, William got to thinking. He wondered why Edina was able to travel back without the potion. He realised she must have been in close contact with Isabel when she collapsed and even just the slightest amount of potion would be transferrable if she had touched Isabel's skin or clothes. And the mystery was solved when Edina told William she tucked Isabel into bed after she had fainted.

"We mustn't get caught," said Jess as they approached the tree. "They'll all think we're witches and probably kill us."

"Let me help," said Edina. "I know where all the keys are, and if you do get caught, I can help you escape."

"Thank you ever so much," replied William. "We'll definitely need your help."

When the children travelled back to 1768, they ran around to the back of the palace. It was quite late, and the darkness made it harder to see their way around. They crept to the store room and peered through the window where Jess had escaped. To their dismay, it was empty.

"Aaah, drats," cried William. "She must be inside the palace. How do we get in without being seen?"

"We must wait," whispered Edina. "Dinner will be served soon, then when the King and Queen are in bed we can enter ."

There wasn't much to do except sit and wait. When King George and Queen Charlotte had retired to their quarters, the candlelight within the palace walls slowly faded. The tallow candles in the kitchen and servants' quarters were put out while the beeswax candles in the chandeliers were extinguished by the servants.

Edina opened a small hatchet and they crept inside. They had to walk very slowly and quietly so their shoes wouldn't echo on the bare floorboards. They tip-toed around the rooms looking for Isabel, but they just couldn't find her. William crept up the stairs and along a narrow corridor. The moonlight shone through the windows, and he was thankful for what little light he had, for he had narrowly avoided walking straight into a small table with a glass ornament on it. That would have been a disaster.

He found his way into a bedroom where the little princes were sleeping soundly. He quietly closed the door and, further down the corridor, found the Queen's quarters. A big frilly dress lay spread out over a lounge and she was fast asleep in her enormous bed, surrounded by pillows made of silk. Two little dogs lay sleeping at the foot of her bed. But there was no Isabel in sight.

When the children had finished searching the palace, they found each other in the kitchen.

"She's just not here," said William. "What do we do now?"

"Do you think she travelled back home?" asked Jess.

"It's plausible, but I don't think so. I would have seen her come home. I just don't get it."

William sat on the big kitchen table. "For the first time in all of my 17 years on this earth, I have no clue where to go now."

William realised that in order to find Isabel, he had to let the palace know he was looking for her. Even if it meant him being captured. Unless he pretended he worked in the palace. He was dressed like everyone else in the palace and there were so many staff it might actually work. So William, Jess and Edina began putting a plan in place.

CHAPTER 12

When the sun rose the following morning, birds began to sing in nearby trees and roosters in the palace garden began to crow. The palace staff slowly woke up and a servant went around the rooms one by one, filling them with light as he lit candles and chandeliers. It would be another couple of hours until the King and Queen would join each other in the dining room for breakfast.

William was up early and tried to look confident, as though he had worked at the palace for years. Edina had dressed him in servants' clothing: long white stockings, a long black coat with gold buttons and black boots. A stiff white shirt sat neatly under the coat. One by one, the staff appeared in the kitchen ready to start work. The cooks set about lighting fires in the big fireplaces, eggs were being beaten, bread was being kneaded, flour tossed around, and trays clanked together as stewards began collecting knives, forks and silverware to lay out on the breakfast table, in readiness for the royal family's breakfast.

When nobody was watching, Edina snuck Jess out of a side door and hid her in the stable yard. Edina knew that the horsemen had finished tending to the horses for the morning and wouldn't be back until lunchtime when the King went riding. Jess found an empty stable, puffed up a little hay into a small mound, sat down and waited.

Edina tended to her usual duties as best she could. William asked her to follow Mr Dankworth as much as possible, in case he happened to mention where Isabel was. She quickly lit the fires in the breakfast and drawing rooms as Mr Dankworth would be arriving at the palace soon. He lived in a cottage on the far side of the palace gardens. A servant in such an esteemed position had the privilege of having his own home and not living in cramped rooms with the servants in the palace. When he arrived, he had his usual scowl plastered across his face. He went straight into the kitchen where a maid poured him a cup of hot tea. Edina stepped into the store room and waited.

Mr Dankworth finished his tea and handed the empty cup to Mrs Splatt, the kitchen manager. He wiped his mouth on a napkin, tugged at the cuffs of his shirt and stomped out of the kitchen. Edina followed him down the corridor to the breakfast room where he inspected the table for the royal family. He peered down at the carefully laid table and lined up the knives and forks. He counted the little jars: honey, strawberry jam and marmalade, yes, they were all there. Edina entered the room and, with her dust cloth, began dusting the furniture. Mr Dankworth looked up directly at her, and she felt his cold stare.

"Sir?"

For a moment, Edina thought Mr Dankworth might ask her the whereabouts of Isabel, or even tell her where she was. But it was not to be.

"His Royal Highness will go riding this afternoon. Have his horse ready at noon."

"Yes, sir." For the first time in her life, she had become part of an adventure, a wonderful, scary and remarkable journey. It was a stark contrast to her unfulfilled life working as a servant. Up at dawn in the chilly mornings and the same routine every day. Seeing how King George and his queen lived made her feel even more dejected, as she knew this was the best she could ever make of her gloomy life. But today she felt alive and happy, knowing that she had just travelled almost 250 years into the future. She wanted not just to be part of it; she wanted all of it. She had already decided to go home with Isabel, Jess and William.

CHAPTER 13

By noon, William and Edina were no closer to finding Isabel. Nobody had mentioned her name. It was as if she was never there at all, which seemed rather peculiar. William spent the morning trying to remain as inconspicuous as possible. He had no idea what was expected of him as a servant, so he stood at the door of the servants' dining room below the stairs where the other palace staff waited to hear the jingle of a bell from upstairs. When Mr Dankworth entered the room, the servants and kitchen staff stood up and pushed their chairs under the table. He stopped and looked directly at William. The cold stare made William feel as though his heart, which was thumping so hard, would burst right out of his chest. He didn't know where to look, so he just looked straight ahead, shoulders back, just like his co-workers. Mr Dankworth looked puzzled and proceeded to walk past everyone and into the boot store, where he picked up a pair of freshly polished riding boots and walked out of the room. Just as William began to relax, Mr Dankworth re-appeared.

"You!" he shouted at William.

Everyone in the room stared at William.

"Who are you? Why have I not seen you before?"

"Errr," stammered William. "I... er... I'm new. Today is my first day."

"What is your name?"

"William Pritchard, sir."

"Pritchard? Hhmmmmm. I don't remember agreeing to your employment at the palace. Who hired you?"

"Me, sir," came a voice. It was Edina. "Queen Charlotte was in need of an extra hand and William has come from the Queen's house in London." William had no idea where the Queen's house was but went along with Edina's explanation. It was clever thinking by Edina, and William thought she was very brave to put her own job on the line to save him.

"Well then, if that is what Her Majesty has requested, then you will see Mrs Jessop, for she will arrange your lodgings, if she hasn't already done so." Mr Dankworth looked William up and down. "And see to it that your shoes are clean every morning before you attend to your duties." And away he went.

"Oh Edina, thank you for saving my skin."

"I beg your pardon, sir? Is there something the matter with your skin? May I help?"

"Ahhh, it's fine, don't worry, just a phrase we use in the 21st century," chuckled William.

Edina blushed.

"Edina, that's such a lovely name," said William. "Where's it from?"

"It's quite ordinary really. It comes from Edinburgh and my ma decided I should be named after the place where I was born."

"So you were born in Edinburgh? I thought I detected a Scottish accent. How old are you?" asked William.

"Eighteen."

"Do you have any family?"

"No, sir. My parents have passed."

"What were their names?"

"Angus and Caitriona Campbell."

"I'm so sorry."

"It's alright. I was a wee child, so I don't remember much about them. My grandmother raised me in the Highlands. That was before she was executed..."

"Executed! Oh my goodness. What happened?"

"They say she was a Jacobite and part of the rebellion. They accused my parents too."

"Oh yes, I've heard of the Battle of Culloden. You mean your family were part of it? How fascinating."

"Aye, tis true but sad. You see, my grandfather was a Jacobite. He fought at Culloden in 1745. He was determined to restore the Stuarts to the English throne, but the English government decided that it should go to their cousins, the Hanoverians, because Queen Anne, who died in 1714, had no successors..." She whispered, "Our king who lives right here is one such Hanoverian. When his grandfather was elected king by the British parliament, some Scots didn't like it. It followed a long period of war between the Scots and the English. When the war finally came to an end at Culloden, my grandparents were executed. It took years for the troops to find them, but they did."

"That is such a sad story." William sighed. "What happened then?"

"I was forced to flee. Had to leave my home and life and I ended up working here. By now I was able to fend for myself. It's not that bad. I got out and now live a life of service."

"Indeed you did get out" said William. "And what a brave lady you are. I just don't know how I would have survived all that."

"But you do" replied Edina. "There's a strength in all of us that keeps us going. We are supposed to live and fight for our place in the world. I'm sure you've fought too, and your spirit will keep on fighting, but in a different way. There's a saying that goes, 'The Scots were born to fight.'"

William was amazed at how a young woman of 18 that had been through so much in life found the strength and determination to make a life for herself, to be a good human being, however hard it was, and all the while be so upbeat and happy.

"I never thought of it like that," said William. "Until now I used to think my life was pretty rotten. I've spent the last few years growing up without my dad and I actually used to think life was tough because I lived in a small house, and oh gosh, Mum worked two jobs and I've never even thanked her for everything she did for Isabel and me. Makes me hang my head in shame."

"Well next time you see your mum, I think you need to tell her how much you love her. If I could have just one hug with my mum..." Edina drifted off deep in thought and William placed his hand on her shoulder.

"I know what you mean. And next time I see my mum, I'll be sure to give her that big hug she deserves. I suppose I should get back to the stables to check on Jess."

The stablehand had just saddled the King's horse and led the horse from the stable and into the yard. As soon as the stablehand turned around to tighten the reins, William scurried into the barn.

"Jess. Are you here?"

Jess sprang up from under a pile of hay. Her hair was covered in strands of hay, and she stood there picking out the little sprigs. "Yuck," she replied. "Yuck... but strangely... warm."

"Any news?"

"Nothing." Jess sighed. "Are you sure she didn't go back through the trees?"

"If I know Izzy, there's no way she would leave you here by yourself. No, I very much doubt she's gone home. She's still here, somewhere. I think we need to start asking the palace staff because we're not getting anywhere."

While Jess waited in the stables, William asked some of the younger servants if they knew of Isabel's whereabouts. After hearing nothing but 'no' or 'you best ask Mr Dankworth', he realised it was time to approach the big scary man himself. He walked around the palace rooms and found him pouring tea for Queen Charlotte. She was entertaining Lady Frances Harpur and the women sat together and gossiped about the King's vision for a new garden at the palace, problems with their servants, their family and children. Queen Charlotte was a wonderful queen to George III. They were happy and she was a good mother to her children. She did not discuss matters of government with her friends or the King, for she found that rather dull and left those conversations to her husband and his ministers.

When Mr Dankworth finished pouring the tea, he bowed and left the room. William followed him down the corridor. "Excuse me, sir."

"What is it?" Mr Dankworth kept walking.

"The girl who was sleeping in the bed upstairs. Do you know where she went?"

Mr Dankworth waved his arm. "Her mother came for her."

"Her mother! What do you mean *her mother*?"

"Young man, do you have a problem with your ears? If I continue to be drawn into this banal conversation, I might just self-combust! Now be off."

Oh no! William thought. *How on earth did Mum come and take her home? How did she find us? Why didn't she take Jess home too?* There had to be a plausible explanation for it. Maybe she was feeling unwell again. William needed more answers; he needed to know for sure. Then he had to get Jess and return home. He swiftly walked towards the kitchen and literally bumped into a servant who was holding a tray full of food. The tray, the servant and William ended up on the floor in one big goopy mess. The servant was none too pleased as he gave William a cold stare.

"I'm terribly sorry," said William as he tried to scoop up the mess from the floor.

"What's all this!" yelled a furious Mrs Splatt.

"It was my fault," replied William. "I'll clean it up. Please leave it." By the time William had finished his sentence, several kitchen staff were on their hands and knees cleaning up the mess. Mrs Splatt instructed the fallen servant to change immediately and summoned another to arrange a new tray. William took the opportunity to ask Mrs Splatt about Isabel.

"Mrs Splatt, the girl who was sleeping upstairs. Did you see her mother who came to collect her?"

"Of course I did. Spoke to her myself and saw them leave together."

"What did she look like? You see, I know the girl and wanted to ensure she was feeling better."

"Well," replied Mrs Splatt. "The girl walked out the front door with her mother, but she looked very pale, and come to think of it, she mostly looked asleep. I just assumed she was still unwell."

"Do you know where they went?"

"Said they were going home to Adrian Hall."

"And the mother? Can you describe her?"

"She had on a long black dress, a black cape, at least I think it was black. Oh, she had long black hair too. Strange woman if you ask me," muttered Mrs Splatt as she trotted off back to the store room.

And in an instant, William knew that his mother had not travelled through the trees to take Isabel back home. For Mother was still at home and had been all along. There could only be one other woman who knew that the Pritchard children were in 1768.

CHAPTER 14

While the Pritchards are a kind, loving and gentle family, it's hard to believe that Isabel and William's aunt is the exact opposite. She is spiteful, revengeful and full of hatred. In the year 1765, Raven had, by accident, travelled to Bishop Richard Terrick's home while she was trying to get back to the 16th century. Bishop Terrick was a kind man who opened his home to her, but when he found out she was a witch he banished her and she disappeared.

When Mother and Raven found Drys in 1550, he had kept the talisman for 500 years. Raven lost the battle and Drys rightfully handed it to Mother. Drys had accumulated so much power from the talisman he was able to overthrow Raven's own powers. Drys told her she would grow old and die by the next full moon. After several weeks passed, a full moon appeared in the sky. Raven tried casting every spell she could think of to stay alive, but Drys's spell was too powerful. On her last night on Earth, Raven walked through a small village and found a barn in a meadow. She looked up at the full moon and knew that this was it, the end of her life was nigh, for she could walk no more. She found a corner in the barn and lay down her old and tired body, closed her eyes and waited to die.

The following morning, the horses and cows neighed and mooed, and the owner of the farm regarded this as something rather unusual when the animals began kicking their hind legs into the stable doors. The farmer wrapped himself in a coat, seized a pitchfork from his back porch and headed towards the barn. When he heaved the big wooden door open, the animals were very agitated, for it seemed they were trying to break out of the barn. Big holes had been kicked into the walls and hay bales had toppled over, which had made quite a mess on the floor.

"Easy! Easy," said the farmer. He cautiously rounded up the animals and let them out into the fields. As soon as the animals were outside, they all bolted as fast as they could. It was very odd, because usually they would hang around the farmer and wait for their morning feed. When they had emptied out, the farmer checked the barn, wondering what on earth had spooked the animals. As he reached the far corner of the barn, he found a black, muddied cloak lying on the floor. He picked it up and inspected it. It was a very thick type of material, like velvet, and as he squinted his eyes, he noticed some hair on it. He picked it off and took a closer look. The hair was grey, and he assumed someone very old had made the barn their home for the night. He didn't think much of it, so he began sweeping the barn and re-stacked the hay bales back against the walls. When he finished, he looked out across his fields and saw his animals grazing at the far end of his land. He scratched his head, looked at the cloak and retreated back to his house, wondering what or who had spooked his animals. He prepared breakfast and just before he sat down to eat, he went back to the barn to check that everything was alright. After a quick look around everything was just as he had left it. The cows and horses hadn't moved from the other side of the paddock either. He thought what a strange lot of animals he owned.

When he returned to his house, he sat at his table and realised his loaf of bread and butter and the little jar of jam was gone. The bottle of milk that he left on the table was also gone.

Raven didn't die that night as Drys's spell only worked while he had the talisman. Of course, Drys didn't know this and when Raven woke in the barn the following morning, she looked around then down at her body. Gone was the old lady that went to die in the barn. She was young and strong. She was back.

After Drys had given the talisman to Elinor, Isabel and William's mother, he was glad to be mortal again. After 500 years of living, he was tired of life, tired of having to move around from village to village and tired of seeing people grow old and die.

He decided to pack up his nomadic life and settle somewhere on the south coast of England. He would live out his days somewhere near a beach where he would take evening walks and enjoy feeling the soft sand slither between his toes. One day as he strode through London on his horse and cart full of his worldly possessions, a young woman walked out of a nearby store. The road was muddy after a particularly heavy rainfall and her foot became stuck in the mud. She lost her balance and fell flat on her face.

Drys saw the woman fall and jumped off his horse. He darted between horses and carts and hurried over to the other side of the road and helped her get back on her feet. Her name was Bridget, and as she wiped the mud from her face, Drys saw the most beautiful woman he had ever seen. Three months later they were married and a son was born the following spring. They named him Osiris.

Osiris was a loving child who played happily with his parents when he wasn't helping them working in their nearby fields. Sometimes he would play for hours and come home with an apple for his father or a rose for his mother. On warm summer days, he liked to lie in the long grass and look up at the blue sky and the fluffy white clouds as they drifted across. He loved to make things and Drys helped him carve a sword from a piece of wood. By the time he was 18, he had made a table and three chairs from a tree that his father had cut down for firewood. When Drys realised that Osiris had a natural talent for crafting, he found him a job as a carpenter and the small house that the family lived in was rebuilt by

Osiris. It had a lovely stone mantel over the fireplace, where Bridget placed flowers that she picked from the garden, and they slept in comfortable beds with a sturdy wooden frame.

However, the beautiful home that Osiris had built with all of the lovely furnishings meant nothing when his mother suddenly passed away. She had just finished buying bread in the village, and on her way home, a tree had fallen and blocked the pathway. The tree was too big to climb over and so she decided to walk through a nearby field to get home. On this particular day, a group of men were practising their archery skills to prepare for the competition at the village fair the following week. They did not see Bridget, for the grass she was walking through was high. An arrow was pointed at the target which was quite a distance away. Francis Evans, who was an expert archer, pulled back the arrow and fired. It hit the target and he pulled another arrow from his sack. As he lined it up and took aim, he stood very carefully, ready to release it. Then all of sudden, a nearby deer heard a crack among the trees, got spooked and ran towards the party. Francis got the fright of his life. He jolted as he released the arrow, and it missed the target. The arrow killed Bridget instantly.

Drys was devastated and became a shell of the man he used to be. The laughter in the house was now gone and the flowers on the mantel had wilted down to dust. And so one morning, Drys woke Osiris and told him he could no longer live at the home that reminded him so much of his beloved wife. He needed to leave for a while. He wasn't sure when he would be back but said they would be reunited one day.

Osiris was now on his own. Every night he sat at the dining table in silence. He looked out of the windows and no longer saw blue skies with fluffy clouds. His days were filled with the cold silence of loneliness, and when the sun set, he went to bed early until he eventually fell asleep. When he woke every morning, it took all his strength to get out of bed. He trudged to the kitchen, with its dusty plates and cups piled up in racks. He no longer lit a fire, and the house was dark and cold.

One day Osiris sat on the front porch and spent all afternoon thinking about life. He then stood up and walked into his bedroom. He packed a small bag and tied it to the reins on his horse and rode away from the house. He didn't even look back. He wasn't sure where he was going or what he was going to do, but he knew that he couldn't live in the house any longer. He travelled during the day and spent his nights sleeping at inns around the countryside. Eventually, he found himself in a small village in the middle of England called Warwickshire. The year was 1580 and Osiris had just turned 25.

Over the years, Osiris found work here and there as a carpenter and soon a new century had begun. The year was 1600 and Queen Elizabeth I had been on the throne for 41 years. Osiris was now 45 years old, and just like his father, he too had not aged. While Drys knew the reason why he had not aged, Osiris did not, for Drys had decided not to tell his own son that he had lived for 500 years. He was completely unaware that Osiris had unwittingly inherited the talisman's power of eternal life.

Osiris had few friends. Just like his father, he didn't spend long in the same village. One afternoon after a dull and lonely day, he walked through his village and stopped at the steps of the church. As he sat and enjoyed the warmth of the sun, a young man approached him.

He was 35 years of age, well dressed, his long brown hair curled neatly under his ears and looked quite fashionable with a goatee and moustache.

"Good sir," said the man.

Osiris looked up to the young man standing in front of him.

"My name is Robert Catesby. I have been informed you are a furniture maker."

"Tis true. I can make anything," replied Osiris.

"I live in the next village and I am in need of a store room for my home."

"Ahhh, yes. I can certainly build a store room. A simple craft, should only take a day or two."

"Can you start on the morrow?"

"Yes."

"Your fee?"

Osiris paused for a moment. "Ten crowns and three shillings."

The young man smiled. "That is a most agreeable fee." He handed Osiris a note with his address written on it. "I shall see you on the morrow. I thank thee and good day to you."

Osiris was pleased that his next month's rent was now accounted for. The following morning, he arrived at the house and began the build for his new client. As he worked, his friend offered lunch, and by the end of the day, they had become friends. Osiris and Robert enjoyed the theatre, and on warm days, they regularly travelled down to London's Globe Theatre to watch the latest Shakespeare play. If they were lucky enough, they would be offered undercover seats around the perimeter of the theatre. If they were late, they had to stand in front of the stage with hundreds of other spectators in rain, hail or shine. Sometimes people would throw rotten food at the more unsavoury characters on stage. A couple of times Osiris got hit in the back of the head by a flying lettuce or tomato. Robert would stand next to Osiris and laugh at his misfortune of being so tall.

In 1604, Robert introduced Osiris to his new friend who had travelled to England from the Netherlands. His name was Guido, and one evening as Robert, Guido, Osiris and several others sat in a small country inn, they gathered around a table and the men began devising a plot to kill King James I. They were planning to blow up the Houses of Parliament when the King would be present at the opening of parliament. As soon as Osiris heard the words 'gunpowder', he knew that this was something he did not want to be a part of. He made a hasty exit and stayed well away from the group, which proved to be a wise decision. In 1605, the plot was uncovered and Guido Fawkes, Robert Catesby and all the other conspirators were caught. They were all executed.

CHAPTER 15

In September 1666, Osiris lived above a bakery in Pudding Lane. After a long day spent lacquering tables, he tidied up the workshop and walked home. That evening he decided to retire early, and at 9 o'clock, he climbed into bed and extinguished his bedside candle. A few hours later, he was woken by people shouting. He thought someone was having an argument, so he put his head under his pillow and rolled over. However, the shouting became louder and when he pricked his ears, there were at least half a dozen voices all shouting over one another. Then he smelt a very odd smell. He sat up and sniffed around. It was a burning smell, and when he hopped out of bed to take a look through his window, his feet felt hot. He looked down and saw little pockets of smoke seeping through the floorboards. Realising that his home was on fire he whipped his clothes on, shoved his bare feet in his boots and bolted. He ran down the timber stairs and out the front door. The bakery that he lived above was on fire and the flames hissed as he watched in utter disbelief.

His landlord, Thomas Farriner, was a baker and thought he had extinguished the flames in his oven at the end of the day, but all it took was a spark. Half of London would burn to the ground. Just about all of the shops and houses in London were built with timber and there was no hope of the fire burning out. The flames spread so quickly that there was nothing anyone could do and the fire raged through London for four days and nights. The hot flames burned everything in its path. Families ran from their homes, and as they ran through the streets to escape the fire, they left behind a trail of destruction and a fog of thick smoke that engulfed the sky. Thousands of people headed straight for the riverbanks and jumped into boats. They rowed down the river and away from the great fire. Mothers and children sat huddled together wrapped in blankets and as they looked back to the city all they could see was the red sky. They watched the city burn while their husbands and sons formed a human line from the river into the city, scooping buckets of water to extinguish the flames. Osiris helped the men do their best to put out the fires and when several days later the wind changed direction, the fires eventually burned out. Osiris was exhausted and covered head to toe in soot.

It was a difficult few years for Osiris and everyone else who lived in London. The bubonic plague had made its way to England for the second time and was spreading rapidly throughout London. Because Osiris had mostly kept to himself, he was lucky enough not to catch it. The only positive thing to come from the great fire of 1666 was that it killed the rats and fleas that carried the disease.

The ensuing cold winter months also halted the spread of the disease.

In the year 1765, when Osiris's peers had long gone, he was still alive. He was 210 years old and still looked like a 25-year-old man. He had become angry and felt that he must have annoyed someone or done something so bad to have this 'thing' happen to him. He grew depressed and one day decided to jump into the River Thames and let the current sweep him away. Early one morning, he walked through the city, past St Paul's Cathedral and over to London Bridge. When he was halfway over the bridge, he looked down at the murky river. He climbed up and sat on the bridge, his hands tightly gripping the edge. He slowly stood up and took a deep breath. As he closed his eyes, he felt something pull him from behind. He fell backwards and landed with a thud on the ground. The shadow stood over him and he realised it was a woman. He blinked several times and raised his arm over his eyes to block the morning sun as and the woman held out her hand. He slowly raised his hand, and she grabbed it, pulling him up. He jolted upright and stood right in front of her.

"I see you're having a bad day," she said.

"Tis true," he replied. "A bad day and a bad life. I cannot go on." He lowered his head with shame.

"It cannot be that bad," she said as she looked him up and down. He did not look like a beggar, for his clothes were clean, and he clearly ate well, for all of his teeth were still in his mouth.

"Come," she said.

Osiris walked off London Bridge with the woman, and together they would form a very dangerous friendship.

CHAPTER 16

It was now the year 1767 and two years since Osiris had met his friend on London Bridge. A new dawn was beginning for Britain called 'The Factory Age'. Manual labour was being replaced by machinery such as Richard Arkright's new yarn spinning machine. Osiris was still very much in demand as a carpenter, and he seemed to find work wherever he went. After all, every house required even the most basic of furniture such as a bed frame, tables and chairs and for the upper class, chests that ladies filled with their lace, perfumes and jewellery. One such lady who owned a fine country home just outside London was Mrs Edwina Sallow. Her husband owned several factories in steel manufacturing, which afforded them a couple of lovely homes in the English countryside and a big shiny black carriage to ride around in. Mrs Sallow had heard of Osiris's carpentry skills and wrote to him requesting that he visit her to build a staircase at her home in the very upper class borough of Mayfair. Two weeks later, Osiris sipped tea with Mrs Sallow as they stood at the bottom of the old staircase, Mrs Sallow expressing her utter dislike of it.

"It's simply hideous," she cried. "It's far too small, and when one opens the front door," she moaned, "one must be privy to a grand entrance, and that, my dear, begins with a grand staircase." As she sashayed back to the drawing room, the shiny white pearls that hung from her neck jangled in tune with her dainty little steps on the carefully polished floorboards.

Mrs Sallow offered Osiris a handsome sum and it was agreed that he would start work on the new staircase the following Monday. Every day Osiris was at the house by 8 o'clock in the morning. He was punctual and efficient, a model worker, as one would say. After six long months of gruelling manual labour, Osiris finally finished the staircase. It was narrow at the top and with each step, the staircase grew wider so that by the time one reached the bottom step, it looked magnificent, taking up most of the entrance hall.

Osiris was proud of the new staircase and couldn't wait to show it off to Mrs Sallow. After having spent the past six months on her country estate, she made the journey down to London to see her new staircase. Osiris had waited at the house since six in the morning and she finally arrived at noon. When the door opened, there stood the grand staircase, its mahogany wood smelling of newly painted lacquer. She produced a pair of glasses from her purse and slipped them over her nose. She walked up the stairs, slowly gliding her hand along the bannister. When she reached the top of the stairs, she turned around and slowly walked back down. Osiris waited patiently at the foot of the stairs watching her face, willing for a positive reaction.

"I like it," she said. "My husband will send your fee promptly."

Osiris was ecstatic. He had never felt so proud and had never worked so hard on anything in his whole life. He celebrated with his friend that evening. They dined at a very expensive restaurant, and he didn't care. The money he had just earned would be enough to buy a plot of land in the countryside. He made plans to build a new home and asked his friend to live with him, for he planned build a house for her too.

However, a week went by and Osiris had not received his payment. He waited another week and, on the third week, wondered if something had happened to Mr and Mrs Sallow. He was worried and thought something awful must have happened to them. His money had completely run out, and if he didn't get paid soon, he would be homeless as well as penniless. So he made the trip to the Sallow home in Mayfair and knocked on the front door. A butler dressed in a fine suit and crisp white shirt opened the door.

"Sallow residence," he said in a very gentlemanly manner. "To whom do you wish to speak?"

"Mrs Sallow," said Osiris.

"She is unavailable," came the reply.

"Then I wish to see Mr Sallow."

"He is unavailable."

"Perhaps you can help," said Osiris. "I have not been paid for the staircase and have been waiting several weeks now."

"Ahhh, yes," said the butler. "I have a message from Mrs Sallow. Mr Sallow has inspected the staircase and does not like it."

Osiris's heart almost fell out of his chest. "Does not like it? What do you mean? Mrs Sallow said she liked it and would pay my fee."

"I am aware of the agreement. However, Mr Sallow does not like it."

"What are you saying?" asked a panicked Osiris. "What does that mean?" Osiris knew exactly what it meant.

"You'll not be paid. Please leave or I shall have no option but to have you removed." The butler shut the door in Osiris's face. He stood on the front porch dumbfounded. He couldn't believe that he had spent six months of his life perfecting a work of art which had ended in this way. He recounted the conversation with Mrs Sallow and he remembered quite distinctly that he would be paid. There was no question of whether Mr Sallow would like or dislike it. There was no question of him not being paid. He banged on the door, but nobody came. The next day, he returned to the house and when he knocked on the front door, again nobody came. After waiting outside the house all day, he eventually gave up and returned home, the home he was about to be evicted from. He sat at his dining table and cried. He just couldn't understand how someone could treat another person that way. He must have sat at the table for hours because he didn't even hear his friend knocking on the door, nor did he hear her footsteps when she opened the latch and entered.

"Oh my!" she said. "What is the matter?"

Osiris told her that he would not be paid for the staircases. He was devastated, and his friend was seething. She would not have her new house built, nor would she own any land. The rage began building from the pit of her stomach.

"We'll see about that!" she spat. "Leave this to me."

"What will you do? What *can* you do?" he asked as he sobbed.

"My dear friend," she said. "As long as I live on this earth, nobody crosses me. Nobody crosses my friends. I can bestow the most abhorrent, abominable, hideous and horrendous affliction on anyone I like."

"How can do you that?" asked Osiris.

"Let me introduce myself properly. When we met, I told you my name was Gudrun. You see, I am also known by the name Raven."

Raven had grown tired of living by herself all these years. She wanted a partner, not a friend, but someone she could manipulate, and when she saw Osiris looking desperate and helpless, she thought he would be perfect. She treated him so kindly by offering her friendship. She cooked meals for him and taught him to play Primero, her favourite card game that was very popular at the time. She lied to Osiris about her life, telling him that she had lovely parents who had unfortunately drowned. She garnered much sympathy from Osiris, cleverly crafting her web of lies and deceit to slowly draw him in to doing anything she wanted.

Osiris never told Raven who his father was and had no idea she had already crossed paths with Drys. Raven was so self-centred that she never once asked about his own family. But that was to be expected of someone like her, for she had higher ambitions. She had no time for pleasantries, they wore her out, but she knew she needed Osiris on her side, so she listened to his stories, nodding her head, pretending to be interested, all the while thinking how utterly boring they were.

Raven told Osiris that the Sallows had to pay for the way they treated him. They set about concocting a plan to seek their revenge on the Sallows. Osiris suggested barging into the house and pulling the staircase apart, but that would be too easy and certainly not in the way Raven operated. No, that wouldn't do, for it had to be nasty and messy.

Something the Sallows would regret for the rest of their greedy lives.

It didn't take long for Raven to devise a plan and when she told Osiris, he felt exhilarated, overjoyed, happy knowing that he would finally have the upper hand. Osiris was ready. He was tired of doing the right thing all the time. Look where it had got him? Penniless and homeless.

Several weeks later, Raven arrived at the Sallow house. She knocked on the front door and the same butler answered it. Her hair was tied up in a neat little bun under a frilly cap and she wore a brown dress that looked akin to a maid's uniform.

"I'm here about the job," she said.

"What job?" asked the butler.

"*The* job," she replied. "I am a seamstress and Mrs Sallow has sent for me."

The butler had no idea what Raven was talking about. For every person who came to work at the house, he was usually informed before they were due to arrive.

Raven sighed and propped her hands on her hips, as though the butler was wasting her time. "Mrs Sallow sent for me. If you have not been notified, then you should go and ask."

"Ask who?"

"Anyone! I don't care who you ask, just go and ask someone."

"Wait here," said the butler. Before he could close the door, Raven was already in the foyer. The butler would normally have insisted she wait outside, but on this particular day he didn't, for he had been offered a new position elsewhere, a better one, and was serving out his notice. He actually didn't care that Raven would be left alone in the house by herself. So off he wandered to find the housekeeper.

When he returned a few minutes later to tell Raven she had been mistaken and Mrs Sallow did not require a seamstress, she was gone. He stood in the hallway and looked around. He opened doors into the adjoining rooms, but she wasn't there either. *How odd*, he thought. He shuffled off and went about his usual daily business.

The next time Mr and Mrs Sallow stayed at their Mayfair home, strange things began to occur. Mrs Sallow was a very vain woman and every time she walked up or down the grand staircase that Osiris had lovingly crafted, her hair began to fall out. It started with a few extra strands when she brushed her hair before she went to bed. The strands turned into clumps and when her head ended up with big bald patches, she sought the help of an apothecary, who mixed up all manner of tonics to rub onto her head. Nothing worked, of course, and by the time

Mrs Sallow was due to attend the next big ball in London, she was completely bald. She tried wearing wigs but they just kept slipping off.

One particular afternoon when Mrs Sallow had arranged to meet some friends for afternoon tea, she had her maid tie ribbons to the sides of her hat so she could tie them under her chin. *Aaaahh, yes,* she thought as she stood in front of her dresser admiring the way she cleverly found a way to leave the house. When the butler opened the front door, she stepped out with her hat tied neatly on her head and stepped into her carriage. She peered out of the window looking smugly at the people walking the streets.

When she arrived at her favourite restaurant in London, she sat down with her friends and chatted as tea was poured. It wasn't long before the maître d' noticed that she was the only woman wearing a hat in the whole restaurant. How very impolite it was. He approached the table and kindly asked her to remove her hat. As he waited, she simply ignored him. After an awkward silence, he said "Ahem." Mrs Sallow threw her napkin on the table and glared at him.

"Please, ma'am," he said. "It is not customary for one to wear a hat indoors."

"I shall do what I please," said Mrs Sallow angrily.

"But ma'am..."

"Get away! Get away from my table and leave me in peace!"

The maître d' was so upset that he grabbed the hat and pulled it. Mrs Sallow threw her arms up to reach the hat, but it was too late. The ribbons gave way and the maître d' stood in the middle of the restaurant with the hat in his hands and a look of utter shock on his face. He was looking down at a completely bald Mrs Sallow. By now everyone in the restaurant was staring in disbelief. Guests had dropped their silver cutlery onto their plates and one man sitting on the adjacent table to Mrs Sallow almost choked on his mutton pie. One of Mrs Sallow's friends fainted in her seat and her other guests didn't even notice she had fainted and was lying under the table, for they were too busy staring at her bald head.

Mrs Sallow had never felt so humiliated in her whole life. The restaurant she was dining in wasn't any restaurant. It was the most expensive restaurant in London and everyone from lords and ladies to the banking elite were regular diners. They all knew Mrs Sallow and by the time she ran to her carriage and sped home, just about all of London's high society was gossiping and laughing at her. Mrs Sallow's smugness had been wiped straight off her nasty face. She withdrew from society and never left the house again.

Mr Sallow, on the other hand, had tufts of thick black hair growing from the pores of his skin. Hair grew from his ears, his nose, and just about every patch of skin was soon covered in hair. People joked that Mrs Sallow's hair had died and grown on her husband's body. They were the laughing stock of London and he left his mansion in Mayfair, with its brand new staircase, and retreated back to his country estate. He stayed within its 20 feet walls until the day he died.

Raven and Osiris often read the newspapers and laughed until they cried when the Sallows were the subject of yet another joke.

"How did you do it?" asked Osiris.

"I am very powerful," replied Raven.

Over the ensuing months, Osiris guessed his best friend was a witch, but he didn't care. He was happy to have a friend, regardless of whether she was a good person or not. Over time the gentle, pleasant and kindly Osiris fell under the spell of Raven. She had turned him into a spiteful, hateful and malicious person. Raven was no longer acting alone. Now the world had two evil forces to be reckoned with.

CHAPTER 17

Raven had kidnapped Isabel from Kew Palace and now William had to find them. He and Jess ran from the palace as fast as they could and away from the palace gardens. They ran down the same road where Isabel had met John Bentley. Carriages and horses galloped up and down the busy road. William had no idea where to start looking. *Who is Adrian Hall?* he kept thinking. *Is he Raven's husband? Relative? Does he even exist or was Raven making it all up?*

William and Jess started asking people in the street if they knew of anyone called Adrian Hall. Some people completely ignored them while others stopped and tried to help, but it was no use, for Adrian Hall wasn't a name anyone in the village of Kew was familiar with.

As the afternoon wore on and the evening shadows of the night began to appear, William decided that Jess had to get home so he could look for Isabel. However, Jess refused to go. She was determined to help find her best friend and as much as William begged her, she flatly refused. So they found a small coffee house and sat near the window. This particular coffee house was full of people from all walks of life, for the idea of sitting in a shop and chatting to friends had become very popular in the 18th century. People mostly went to catch up and chat, for the coffee was quite a new concept and it tasted disgusting. William ordered two coffees and they were served in metal cups. Thick and syrupy, William took a small sip and almost spat it out. Jess decided not to drink any of hers after watching William's awkward facial expressions as he swallowed it down. It was like an awful-tasting medicine.

Men and women sat at tables chatting. The men wore big white wigs, and the women wore the loveliest dresses full of bright colours. When they sat down, their dresses were so big and puffy it was difficult to move past them without stepping on them. But somehow the ladies managed.

"What do we do now?" asked Jess.

"We've asked just about everyone in the street."

"We must have asked at least 50 people."

"I just don't know what to do next," said William.

Then Jess stood up on her chair and yelled "Excuse me, please!"

All of a sudden, the conversations stopped, and everyone looked at Jess as though she was from another planet.

"I'm sorry for the interruption, but we are wondering if anyone knows a man called Adrian Hall." Jess looked around at all the faces staring back at her. "Anyone?" she repeated. "Please think carefully as we have lost someone very special and believe she is with someone who goes by the name Adrian Hall."

A man from the back corner stood up. "My dear," he said in a very upper-class accent. "The person you are referring to, this Adrian Hall, simply does not exist."

"We were told he does," cried Jess.

"Well," said the man. "Adrian is not an English name. In fact, Adrian is a Roman name from the town of Hadria, which if I am correct, and I know I am, was a town in Roman times."

Jess and William thought the man was crazy. "Well, thank you for your time," said a forlorn Jess as she sat down feeling very embarrassed.

"However!" came the voice again. "I believe you incorrectly heard the name Adrian Hall and your source, or sources, actually meant to say Hadrian, not Adrian."

"Hadrian?" said William.

"Oh, my dear boy. Must I spell it out? Your friend has gone to Hadrian's Wall. Tis near the border of England and Scotland."

"That's it!" cried William. "Raven has taken her to Hadrian's Wall. It's not a person; it's a place! We heard it wrong."

"Let's go!" said Jess excitedly. "Let's get our Izzy back." When the children ran out of the coffee house Jess stopped at the front step, turned around and ran back inside. She walked straight over to the gentleman and planted a kiss on his cheek. "Thank you!" She walked back past the stunned customers and out of the shop. While the man pretended to be quite disgusted, he felt a warm glow fill his cheeks. He was actually quite happy that he was able to help.

CHAPTER 18

It took almost a week for William and Jess to reach Hadrian's Wall. They had walked, snuck on the back of wagons and stagecoaches and slept in sheds with horses, cows and goats for company. They ate fruit and vegetables from farms and fields and drank water from brooks and streams. The final couple of hours of their journey took them to a small village where the wall began. With 85 miles of wall to cover, they had a lot of walking to do. While William had been used to living rough, Jess was not, and she found it difficult walking in a dress. By the time they had reached the wall, she had removed all of the layers of petticoats and frills from under her dress and torn off the bottom. They kept the extra layers to use as bandages in case of an emergency, so she tied them to her dress like little ribbons.

The wall was built by the Romans in the 2nd century AD. During the Roman conquest, the wall would have looked magnificent. The walls were built six metres high with forts situated along the path where Roman soldiers guarded their territory. But now it was a crumbling wall where whole sections had been removed over the years by people who built their own houses from the large stones. As the children walked alongside the wall with tufts of grass sprouting from the ground, William thought how it would have looked 1600 years ago. He imagined all of the Roman soldiers spread out along the wall, in their red skirts held together by lappets, their shiny helmets they called Galea, and metal armour around their torsos. All of this heavy armour would have been very uncomfortable, and William was glad he didn't have to travel back to Roman times. At least the 18th century wasn't that far away from the modern-day life he was used to. He did, however, think that life in the Georgian era would have been much easier had they invented cars, but a bumpy ride on a horse and, if you were lucky enough, a stagecoach, would have to do for the time being.

Knowing that Raven and Isabel would now be somewhere close by, William and Jess began asking local farmers if they had come across someone matching the descriptions of Raven and Isabel. After hearing so many 'no's, they were surprised when a potato farmer answered 'yes'. The farmer's name was Mr Boone and he recounted the story of how he heard a knock on his door late one night. He lit his bedside candle and when he opened his door, a woman and a young girl were standing on his doorstep. They looked very tired and hungry, so the farmer's wife, Mrs Boone, made up a bed and gave them some food before they all retired for the night. It didn't take long until Raven and Isabel were fast asleep. When the Boones woke the following morning, their guests were gone, along with the blankets from the bed and half the food they had in their store room. As they stood in their small lounge room wondering why their guests would steal from them, Mr Boone noticed scratch marks on the kitchen table. He pulled his glasses from his pocket, and upon closer inspection, he realised they weren't scratch marks but an engraving which read 'help carlisle cast...'

He quickly got dressed, hopped on his horse and rode off looking for his guests. After riding 10 square miles without a trace of them, he realised they were indeed gone, so he returned home. With Mrs Boone waiting anxiously for any news, they presumed their guests had disappeared forever and wouldn't see them again.

The Boones were very glad to see William, for they worried about the message on the table and what it meant. William explained that the girl was his sister and the woman his aunt. Mr Boone showed William the message on the table, but they still couldn't work out what it meant. Mrs Boone insisted the children have a proper meal and a hot bath before they continue their journey, and later that afternoon, William and Jess were on their way again with clean clothes and a belly full of food which was mostly potatoes grown straight from the farm. When they reached the main road, Mr Boone ran out of his house. "I know what it means!" he shouted at the children. "Carlisle!"

"What's Carlisle?" asked William.

"It's a town. Carlisle is a town not more than a day's walk from here."

"Fantastic! Thank you!" they shouted back.

"Carlisle," chirped William. "We're heading in the right direction. We'll be there tomorrow."

"I'm glad, really glad," replied Jess. "I just want Izzy to be safe and I'm grateful we met that farmer because we also know she's alive."

That night when Jess was fast asleep under a tree, William worried about seeing Raven again. He wondered how he would approach her, what he would say to her and how he would successfully remove Isabel from her clutches. Maybe Raven was expecting him, perhaps that was why she took Isabel. But why? There wasn't any point spending all night thinking about it, so he nestled down next to Jess and slept.

CHAPTER 19

After being woken by birds chirruping in the trees, by lunchtime the children had finally reached Carlisle. Walking alongside Hadrian's Wall, the castle tower came into view. William pictured Isabel scratching 'cast' on the farmer's table and he marvelled at how clever and resourceful she was. If it hadn't been for her quick thinking, William would have no idea where to find her, but now he did know where to find her and he was going to get her back.

Carlisle Castle was an old Roman castle which lay on the banks alongside the River Eden. Once a fine residence for kings and queens, Mary Queen of Scots was the last monarch to use it as a royal residence in 1567. The castle was once full of life filled with royal courtiers, soldiers, servants and residents who held various jobs for the Crown. Once upon a time, music would have filled the halls in the evenings as banquets of food were served every day. Now the old ruins stood silent and dilapidated since it was now a home to the odd traveller or a wild animal looking to shelter from the cold winter months. William wondered what secrets the castle held in order for Raven to travel all that way with Isabel. It wouldn't be long before he'd find out.

They walked up the grass hill to the big wall that surrounded the tower. After finding the entrance, they found themselves in the courtyard.

"We need to stick together," said William. "Raven is capable of anything."

"Sure can do," quipped Jess.

"Look, Jess, I appreciate you want to help, but really, you don't know Raven, and she is very nasty, so you need to do what I say and understand the danger we're facing."

"I understand, Will. To be honest, I'm just as scared as you are, probably a thousand times more, and when my scared feelings come to the surface, my big mouth gets the better of me."

"It's okay to feel scared. Just know that I'll be looking out for you. We have only one mission here, to get Izzy home safely."

"Where do we start?" Jess looked around at all the little paths that led away from the courtyard into the castle.

"Over there." William noticed a doorway where a flicker of light shone from within. Just inside the door, a spiral staircase went downwards. All they could see was half a dozen stairs then it became completely dark. The light they had seen was a candle which was perched in a welt on the wall.

William pulled it from the wall and began walking down the stairs very carefully. Jess walked right behind him and clutched onto the back of his shirt. The further down the stairs they walked, the colder it got, and they soon realised they were in the dungeons. Small rooms with big iron bars filled the cold, musty space. The walls were full of carvings. Etched into the rock were pictures of animals: deer, sheep, horses to name a few, along with carvings of flowers, shields and keys. He thought the prisoners must have engraved the pictures to relieve themselves from boredom.

"Come on," whispered William. "Nothing down here. Let's go back upstairs."

"With pleasure," replied Jess.

They walked through the great hall where a large banqueting table sat in the middle of the room. Scraps of paper, half a dozen books, empty bottles of black ink and broken quills were scattered on the table and onto the floor. Some of the bottles had been smashed and shards of glass were strewed around the table. Jess picked up a broken bottle and scooped her finger around the rim where the ink had dried up from many years gone by. William picked up a book and dusted it off. He flicked through the pages and realised it was a military book that contained the names of hundreds of Scotsmen. Indeed they were, for they were the names of the Jacobites who fought at the battle of Culloden. William flicked through the pages and thought of the story Edina told him about her grandparents. He wondered whether their names were in the book. Carlisle Castle was used as a garrison during the battle and many of the captured Jacobites were imprisoned in its dungeon, where William and Jess had just been.

"It doesn't look like anyone's here," said Jess.

"Wait! I heard something!" William motioned for Jess to keep silent. "Sounded like it was coming from outside," he whispered.

William walked quietly to a nearby door and looked up. Above the tower, the feathery white clouds very quickly turned dark grey. A gust of wind blew around the bottom of the tower, blowing William and Jess towards it. William tried to grip his feet firmly on the ground, but the wind was too strong, for his whole body was being pushed by some incredible force towards the tower. No matter how hard he fought his body to retract, it was no use. He turned the other way around and pushed his arms out in front of him, but the wind became more ferocious and swung him around again. Jess fell to the ground and tried getting up.

"Stay down!" shouted William as he saw her struggling. "Don't move!"

Jess did exactly what William said and sat on the stone pavement. She curled up into a ball and put her head between her legs.

Then all of a sudden, the wind stopped. It was as if a tornado had ripped through a city. Tufts of grass, loose stones and weeds now littered the courtyard.

"Are you okay?" asked William.

"What *was* that?"

"*That* was Raven."

CHAPTER 20

Two thousand years ago, a group of Romans invaded England. On a patch of land in Carlisle, near the Scottish border, they built a fort made of timber and rock to protect themselves from invasion. Shortly afterwards, a settlement of people called the Luguvalium built on the land around the fort. The Luguvalium people were fiercely protective of their land and their possessions, for they didn't own much and everything they had was extremely valuable. Some had cows that were their main source of income and others sold wood in order to feed their families. This meant that if the cow didn't produce much milk or if the winter weather was so cold that it proved impossible to cut down trees, it meant there was very little food to eat. So when a builder who lived in the village found a shiny gold key in the excavations of the plot that would become Carlisle Castle, he swiftly hid it in his shoe and continued working.

That night he showed the key to his wife, and as they sat around the dinner table, they contemplated what it was for and how long it had been there. They realised it must have belonged to someone, but they had no idea who. Perhaps it was a Roman soldier, or a king who was in the area passing by and lost it during his travels. Either way, they held onto it knowing that one day they could sell it, if indeed it was made of gold. The builder was instrumental in the building of a new castle and thought a good place to hide the key was among the stones under the stairs that led into the dungeons. He cut a small hole and stretched his arm as far as he could. He gently placed the key as far as the tips of his fingers could reach and let go. He had planned to leave the village with his family the following summer and would come back to fetch the key when he was ready to leave.

The key sat among the stones throughout winter, and in early spring, the builder began making plans to move away from the village. By now, the castle was almost finished being built, and late one night the builder returned to the castle to retrieve his gold key. He walked very slowly down the stairs leading to the dungeon, for it was dark and, just like William and Jess had found, the further he walked, the darker it became. Halfway down the stairs, a loose rock gave way and buckled underneath him. In the darkness, he lost his footing and fell the rest of the way to the bottom of the stairs. The pain shot right up his legs and he let out an almighty scream. But nobody heard him. He couldn't stand up. He couldn't even heave himself up the stairs using his arms. As he lay on the cold stone floor of the castle that he helped build, he wondered what to do.

He was in so much pain that he didn't hear someone walking by the top of the stairs and that person didn't realise an injured man was all alone in the dungeon, so the door was swiftly shut, which signalled the end of the builder's life. He died trying to retrieve his gold key from under the stairs. And so the key remained in that crevasse under the stairs of the dungeon.

Inside the tower, Raven sat on a chair at the end of a long wooden table and waited. She felt like a queen sitting on her throne. A throne befitting for a witch, for it was not covered in luscious red velvet, nor was it adorned with jewels. Raven, swathed in her black robes, sat quietly and waited.

William had spent the last week preparing himself for his encounter with Raven but, when he did see her, was quite shocked to see her sitting on her wooden throne when he entered the tower. He felt a little weird when he locked eyes with Raven. He didn't feel scared, nor did he feel anxious. He felt strong, powerful, and saw Raven in a completely different way than he had when she went through the trees with his mother to find Drys. Back then he was petrified, but this time he felt strong.

"Alright, where is my sister?" he said angrily.

"Ahhhh, William," replied Raven. "So nice to see you again. Oh! I see you have a friend. How nice."

Jess nervously clutched William's hand.

"Leave her alone. Where is Isabel and why have you taken her?"

"So many questions! It's rather exhausting. Firstly your sister is alive, and I have taken her because she has something that belongs to me."

"The amulet," said William.

"Maybe." Raven stood up and walked over to Jess. "And who are you?"

"I'm Jess, Isabel's best friend," Jess said defiantly. "I'm not scared of you."

Raven stood right in front of Jess until their noses were almost touching. "Boo!" she hissed.

Jess jumped and William pulled her behind him.

"I want something which will make me richer and more powerful than anyone in the whole entire world."

"And what would that be?" asked William.

"If you want Isabel back, she has to get something for me, but she's being ever so silly and refusing, which is why you can't have her back until she does what she's told."

"What do you need from her? I'll do it instead. Just name it and I'll do it."

"Go ask her yourself. She's here somewhere. You'll just have to find her." Raven cackled and sat back down on her big wooden chair.

"Fine," said Jess. "That's just what we'll do. Come on, Will."

The children looked around and saw a staircase behind Raven. They walked cautiously around the table, well out of Raven's way, and towards the staircase. They climbed the spiral stairs and found themselves at the top of the tower. They glanced around the grounds of the castle below and decided that Isabel was most likely somewhere inside the castle. When they returned to the bottom of the stairs, Raven was still sitting in the chair. The smirk on her face told William she was loving every minute of the game she was playing. They ran past Raven, back through the castle and began searching the bare rooms. They had already been in the dungeons, and they were empty, so they wondered where on earth Isabel could be if the dungeon was the most likely place to keep someone captive.

They scrambled into all of the rooms until Jess heard faint noises coming from behind a wall in a room that had most likely been used as a bedroom, for it was enormous and had large windows.

"Izzy!" she yelled. "Izzy, is that you?" She placed her ear against the wall and stood quietly. Her heart thumped as she waited for a sound, a shout, anything. *Tap tap*. There it was again.

"William!" she screamed. "William!"

William ran into the room puffing and panting. "What is it?"

"I heard a noise from behind this wall. I think it's her."

William looked up at the wall and ran his hands across the wood-panelled surface. He gently pushed at small intervals until they heard a creak. He pushed harder and, just like that, part of the wall opened.

"It's a hidden door," he said. "Very well hidden." He poked his head into the darkness and realised they needed light in order to see where they had to go so he opened the door wide open to let in some natural light. It was enough, for he could see down the tunnel.

"Grab my arm," he told Jess.

They stepped into the tunnel, keeping their backs against the cold wall. The further they walked, the darker it got, until they saw a flickering light ahead. They continued further until they came to what looked like an ante room. In the corner sitting with her head curled up against her knees was Isabel.

"Izzy!" William ran over and threw his arms around his sister. She looked up and into William's eyes. Her voice crackled as she spoke. "You came."

"We need to get you out of here," said Jess as she bent down next to Isabel and took her hand.

"I thought I was going to die here." The tears fell down Isabel's cheeks as she let out a huge cry.

"You're alive and you're safe," said William.

"I can't leave," cried Isabel.

"What do you mean?"

"Raven said something about a key and I am the only one who can find it."

"A key? What key?"

"She knew this was going to happen, that you and I would be here together," Isabel continued "There's a key hidden somewhere in this castle, and it's somehow tied to our family. Only I can locate it. She said I was 'the only one'."

"The only one? What does that mean?" asked William.

"I don't know. That's all she said. She'll kill me unless I get it for her. I refused to do it because I knew as soon as I found it, she'd kill me anyway."

"Good thinking, sis. That decision has probably kept you alive. Listen, we'll talk about that later. For now, we need to get out of here, because Raven is in the tower, and she'll be looking for us." He scooped his little sister up and they walked back through the tunnel against the cold wall and back into the room.

"I knew it was her all along," wept Isabel. "Remember that feeling I've been having the past couple of months at home? That time when I felt someone had pushed me outside the flower shop. It was her. And when Jess and I went to take the amulet to the King, I had that feeling too. Creeping around like she does. Remember I told you about that, Jess?"

"Hang on, Izzy," replied William. "Are you saying that she's been to 2014 and has been following you?"

"Yes! She admitted it. She's been trying to find the amulet too. But of course, she couldn't find it because we didn't even know where it was."

"This is really bad." William sighed. "It means she's probably been following us everywhere, to school, home. It also means we're not safe anymore. Even when we get home, we're not safe because she can find us."

"And how *do* we get home?" asked Jess.

"Let's just concentrate on getting out of this horrible castle first," replied William.

They very carefully walked through the courtyard, dodging all of the stones and debris that Raven had caused, and towards the castle entrance. However, something wasn't right. Just walking out of the castle seemed too easy, and it was, for standing right in front of them at the gates of Carlisle Castle was Raven.

"Let us pass," said William.

"Only when I have what I came for."

"The key? How do I know you won't kill us after we find it?"

"You have a choice," said Raven. "You get me the key and you Pritchards can live."

"Pritchards?" Jess's heart sank.

"And Jess!" demanded William. "She comes with us too."

"Oh no! My dear, darling nephew. She stays with me."

"Noooo!" cried Jess. "Please let me go with them," she begged.

"This is my one-time offer. You get the key and live or you don't get it and you *all* die."

"We can't leave Jess here. What could you possibly want with her?" asked William.

"I won't agree to it!" shouted Isabel.

"She'll kill us all," cried Jess. "You have to do it."

William fumed at Raven. "You are pure evil, and I cannot believe that we are related."

"Ha ha," laughed Raven. "Now, get your sister to stop drivelling and head to the dungeon. She needs to climb into the wall under the staircase. She knows what to do."

William led Isabel towards the castle. "Don't worry," he whispered. "I'll think of something. The three of us are going home together... today."

Isabel and William stepped down the winding staircase and into the dungeon. Under the stairs, she found a small opening where a section of stone was missing. She looked through the crack and sighed. "I can't stretch my arm through there. It's too small."

"You can do it, Izzy. Just squeeze your shoulder in the crack as much as it will go. Your arm will fit."

Isabel stretched as far as she could into the small hole and squeezed her shoulder inside. Her neck was also stretched right up against the crack in the wall. She scraped her hand along the inside of the wall until the sound of something clanked onto the stone. She stretched out her fingers and felt around the tiny space.

"Got it!"

"Easy does it. Whatever you do, don't drop it. Just take your time."

Isabel placed the palm of her hand flat over the key and clenched her fingers around it. With the key firmly in the grip of her hand, she slowly pulled her arm out of the small space.

William held her as she stepped away from the stairs. She handed William the key and rubbed her arm, for it was cold and dusty and a shiver went down her spine. The shiny gold key had a big rectangular lock at one end, and at the handle, a trio of hearts intertwined with each other.

"It's really heavy," said William. "I think it's solid gold. Maybe that's why Raven wants it."

"We can't just hand it over ," said Isabel. "She won't let Jess come home with us."

"Don't worry, I have a plan. It's not a great plan, but it might just work."

William and Isabel then returned to Raven.

"Before I hand over the key," said William, "I want to know why you want it and what it has to do with our family."

"Let me see it first," replied Raven.

William opened his hand and held it up in the sunlight. Raven's eyes lit up. She stared at it; her eyes almost became hypnotised by it.

"There," he said as he swiftly put it back in his pocket. "Now start talking."

"Very well then. If you want to know, then you shall. The key opens a chest. In the chest is a book that holds a very powerful secret. I was there when Drys gave your mother the talisman, along with the amulet. I need the talisman, the amulet and the book."

"And why is that?" asked William.

"Thanks to your stupid sister. She gave the amulet to King George. It has come to my attention that the amulet and talisman together have the power to make the holder of them very ill and are not intended to be kept by one person. You will certainly die. I don't want to die, not ever, and the book is what you might call a book of spells, if you like."

"And where is this chest then?" asked William.

"Oh, I'm not telling you that! Do you think I'm stupid? Giving away all my secrets? Pfft!" said Raven as she waved her hand away.

"You know, the parallels between you and my mother are staggering. She's a really good person and you are just the opposite, a complete monster" said William.

"It's your mother who made me this way. She chose to live a normal life, to abstain from using her power and witchcraft. She could have lived forever. *We* could have lived forever together!"

"And do what? Spend eternity going through the trees terrorising people you don't like? She chose to be mortal to live a decent life, to love and be loved."

"Yeah, yeah, family is everything, blah blah blah."

"It is! If only you knew how it feels to be part of a family, for them to look out for you and have your back. And when things are bad, there's always someone there for you."

"Just like your dad, eh?" Raven laughed.

"Although Mum can't bring Dad home from 1851, she will find a way. She's waiting, we're all waiting for it to happen. It *will* happen! We just need to be patient. We are still very much a family, whether he's here or there, and he knows we're waiting to bring him home."

As soon as William had finished talking, Raven went quiet. It was as though she felt saddened by what he had said about family and love. Perhaps it was something she genuinely yearned for but never had the opportunity to feel it. That was her own doing, for she had chosen her own path in life. She, too, could have lived as a mortal, just like her sister, but she chose power over everything. Her shoulders fell and her whole body softened. It was the first time William had seen her in this way, and for a brief moment, he felt a little sorry for her.

"Here's the key." William held the key above his head and twisted it ever so slightly so that it sat in his hand under the glare of the sun. He held it still while Isabel pulled a piece of broken glass from her sleeve. Standing behind William, she held it up to the sun, and all of a sudden, the sun's glare reflected onto the glass behind the key. It was blinding and Raven couldn't see anything. She raised her arm to block the glare and William threw the key over her shoulder and bolted the other way. He knew the key would mean more to her than catching him. She spun around and all of the children were gone.

"Noooooooo!" she screamed. "You little wretches! I'll get you!" She scrambled on her hands and knees looking for the key. When she found it lying on the stone path, she scooped up the key and rubbed it down with her sleeve. She was furious, more incensed than she had ever been in her entire life. The children had tricked her, and she hadn't expected it.

She held her head up to the sky and shouted:

> "The fleshy mortal,
> one of three,
> shall nay home to nest,
> shall never be free."

Raven shouted it over and over again until she fell to the ground, exhausted. As she lay in the grass, she looked up as the clouds danced across the sky. *You Pritchards will never be free from me.* She had her key, but it wasn't enough. She had been duped, tricked, conned and she couldn't believe how stupid she was to fall for it. The children had escaped, and she decided to bide her time. For now.

CHAPTER 21

When the children passed the Boones' farm on their way back to London, they stopped by to let them know that Isabel was safe and well. William instructed them not to let Raven back into their home and to keep their doors locked at all times. Upon finding out that the children had no transport in which to travel back to London, Mr Boone wanted to help. He told the children that a weekly horse drawn postal service delivered mail from Edinburgh to London, and if they waited for two days, they might be able to get a ride as his brother happened to be the driver of the mail service. And so the children waited. The mere thought of having to find their own way back to London was harrowing, for they had no money and would most likely have to walk, which would take weeks.

During their time on the farm they fed chickens, collected eggs and milked cows. Isabel and Jess learned how to make bread and butter pudding and it tasted sweet and delicious. The two days went quickly, and on Wednesday morning, they waited at the front of the house for the coach to arrive. The driver was more than happy to take the children to London for he was glad of the company, and after a very bumpy ride, they had arrived at Trafalgar Square a few days later. All they had to do now was get to Kew Gardens and find their tree. But it wasn't going to be as easy as that. It never is easy for the Pritchard children.

As soon as they set foot on the palace grounds, they were captured by King George's guards, who had been expecting them. This time the King wasn't in such a jovial and hospitable mood. Mr Dankworth had told the King that Isabel was a witch. The King didn't believe it at first, but when Mr Dankworth told him he would prove it, he reluctantly agreed to find out if there was any truth to the matter.

The children were surrounded by horses and guards and had nowhere to run. They were so close to their tree, for it was just a few feet away. The thought of going home swiftly faded away as the children were ushered back into the palace and locked in the library. They sat in stony silence, hungry and tired after their long journey from Scotland. William looked around the library and detected a rather unusual smell. He followed the smell of linseed and oil to the other side of the room. Sitting on a large wooden easel sat a freshly painted picture of King George III. He put his nose right up to the painting and the fumes that filled his nose made his eyes water. He realised the picture had recently been painted as the shiny painting still looked wet and he looked closely at the brush strokes. Rich gold colours were used to paint the King's robes and a silver spotted sheepskin was draped neatly over his shoulders. And sitting around the King's neck sat the amulet.

"No way!" said William.

"What is it?" cried Isabel. She quickly hopped up from the sofa and joined William.

"Look at this! It's the amulet!"

"It's the painting Jess and I saw in 2014. *The* actual painting!"

"And this painting is the reason we returned the amulet," said William.

"The King had the painting done after you gave him the amulet when we were at the castle," interrupted Jess.

William wondered how the amulet came to be in the painting and now he had the answer.

"It's incredible how this painting has happened because of us," said William. "I mean, the King probably had the painting done because he wanted to wear the amulet and this actual painting will sit in this room for at least the next 250 years."

"Because of us!" squealed Jess.

"Let's not get too excited," said William. "We're on his bad side at the moment."

As the children stood marvelling at the incredible chain of events that led to the existence of the painting, a clunking of keys rattled at the door, and it swiftly opened. Mr Dankworth entered the room with the King behind him. Mr Dankworth sarcastically smiled at the children while the King looked very agitated and instructed the children to sit down.

"Not you," he said to Isabel. "You will stay there." He walked over to her and instructed her to move her hair away from her shoulders. When she did, Mr Dankworth pointed to her neck. The little birthmark was visible just under her ear. There was no use in disputing this, for the fact remained that he had seen it then and he had seen it now. The secret was out. A trusted servant and advisor in the King's court knew that Isabel was that same girl who had saved the King from drowning.

"Do you see it?" asked Mr Dankworth.

"I do," replied the King. "Tis a most unfortunate situation you have found yourselves in," he said to the children. "Mr Dankworth has made me aware of the mark on your neck. While this is not an extraordinary circumstance, what I do find intriguing is that, if my memory serves me right, and indeed it does, this is the same mark of the young girl who rescued me from the pond in years gone. Now tell me the truth. Are you that same girl?"

Isabel started shaking. William stood up. "Please, Your Highness, I can explain."

"Sit down!" yelled Mr Dankworth.

The King motioned to Mr Dankworth. "You may leave. Have the guards posted outside the door."

Mr Dankworth was aggrieved that he couldn't stay to see the children be thrown into the dark, gloomy cellars, for he relished in other people's misery. He begrudgingly bowed his head and walked out of the room, closing the door behind him.

The King studied the children standing before him. He wondered how Isabel didn't age at all while he had grown from a child to a man. Scratching his head, he paced the room back and forth and wondered if they were indeed witches, which would be most unfortunate, for he knew what the public did to witches. Maybe Isabel had some sort of disease whereby she simply stopped growing. Perhaps it was nature that had dealt Isabel that life or perhaps it was something she ate? Or something she did not?

"I cannot fathom it," he muttered. He walked over to his newly painted portrait and contemplated the amulet. "I am not sure what to do with you," he said to the children. "I am not sure what to make of all of this, yet a decision must be made."

"Please, Your Highness." William stood up from the sofa. "May I speak?"

"You may, if it will help your case."

"We are good, honest people, not from around here but we are just passing by. We mean you no harm. We all admire and respect you. You certainly won't believe the truth, but I'll tell you anyway. We are not witches. We are from another time. We have come from the year 2014 and we are able to travel through time."

The King wasn't sure whether to laugh or be very angry at being taken for a fool.

"You talk about respect," he replied as he continued pacing the room, "yet you tell lies of being from the future. Not only is what you say utter nonsense, but you show no respect for the person to whom you are talking."

"It's true! We don't know why it happened to us, but it has, and that's the truth. How do you know that we are lying if you have no knowledge of what lies in the future?"

"You are all liars!" The King was angry.

"Didn't my sister save you from drowning when you were a boy?"

The King said nothing.

"If she was a witch, then she would have drowned too! Aren't witches supposed to drown when thrown into water? Isn't that what they do to them to see if they are lying or not?"

The King folded his arms across his chest but still said nothing. He was clearly deep in thought, for William had a very good point.

"Then let me show you this." William slipped his hand into his shirt and pulled a strip of tape off his bare chest. He carefully peeled the tape away from the note, trying not to tear it. He opened the note and held it up to the King.

The King took the note and looked at it. On one side of the brown note was a picture of Queen Elizabeth II.

"Tis not English currency," he said.

"But it is," replied William. "This woman is *our* Queen, your relative!"

"I don't believe it!"

"It's true. This is a 10-pound note from the year 2014 and our current monarch has been on the throne since the 1950s."

The King flipped the note over several times and gazed upon the picture of Queen Elizabeth.

"This is our longest serving queen and you, Your Highness, will be our longest serving king."

The King was quite taken with the note. He turned it over and studied the other side.

"That's Charles Darwin," said William. "He's a geologist from the 19th century." William waited for the King's response.

"Well then," said the King. "I am still not sure if I believe you. You have provided me with evidence, yet I find it too incredible to believe. And what of this coin that you have given me? What does it represent and why have you given it to me?"

"Your Highness, if I may." William held out his hand and the King realised that he wanted the amulet. He turned around and William slipped it off his neck very gently. "Do you see this?" William pointed to the tiny engraving that read:

> "A jewel of gold
> the passage of time
> in two hands
> doth break the line"

"This inscription refers to the bond between my mother and her sister. You see, we thought it belonged to us, but Isabel saw your painting right here in this room in 2014 and saw the amulet around your neck. We had no idea why you had it, but we thought it should be returned to you, for whatever reason that may be. We felt that it rightfully belongs with you."

William dared not tell the King of the amulet's special powers. The fact that it granted eternal life for his mother and Raven if they spoke the magic spell while holding it together. He wasn't sure if this spell only worked for certain members of his own family or whether it granted eternal life for anyone who said the magic spell. In any case, he wasn't about to tell the King, for he was in enough trouble already.

"Tis quite remarkable," said the King, "how this amulet is so important that you travelled back to give it to me."

"But you see it *does* belong to you and we have returned it to you knowing that when we travel through time, our journey is actually quite dangerous."

"Your Highness, we have risked our lives to return it," said Isabel. "We have parents who are waiting for us to come home. Please, will you let us go home?"

"This business is giving me an awful pain in my head," replied the King. "You still have not proved to me that you are not witches. I am to take my daily rest now and you will stay here until I make my decision regarding this whole sordid mess."

As the King stomped towards the door, he hesitated and turned to William.

"If you have knowledge of future events, tell me then, will I make a good king?"

"Yes, Your Highness, indeed you will," replied William. "You will become instrumental in creating Kew Gardens with Joseph Banks. The gardens will become world famous for its research in plants and trees."

"Will my marriage with Queen Charlotte be a happy one?"

"Indeed it will. Very happy and long-lasting. You will have a lot of children. A lot!"

Shaking his head, the King muttered "Nonsense" under his breath as he left the room.

The library door was shut and bolted, and the guards waited outside. William knew there was no way they could just walk out and go home. They were at the mercy of the King and whatever decision he would make regarding their predicament.

CHAPTER 22

"What will we do now?" asked Isabel. "Does this mean we can't get home?"

"I don't know," replied William. "We'll just have to sit and wait."

Before William had finished his sentence, Jess was at the windows trying to open them. One by one, she pushed them this way and that. Then Isabel was over at the windows rattling them too.

"Come on!" she muttered. "Open!" It was no use. The windows were locked. When the girls realised they were unable to escape through the windows, they flopped themselves on the sofa and waited.

"We need to find out about the key," said William. "We know a bit about the amulet's history, but we know nothing of this key that Raven kidnapped you to get it."

"I agree," replied Isabel. "She made me travel all the way up to the borders of Scotland for it."

"The question is, why you? Why not another little girl your size, that she could have found in the vicinity of the castle. I mean, what makes *you* so special?"

Isabel began to feel rather worried. "Exactly. Why me? It's got to do with our family history. Maybe there's something Mum hasn't told us."

"This just gets more exciting!" squealed Jess. "I can't believe all of this is happening. That I, Jess nobody, is best friends with Izzy, someone who gets kidnapped by a witch to go fetch a key out of a very small spot in a castle. Near Scotland!"

"There's got to be something we don't know. And it's big, I know it is," said William.

"I guess we won't find out until we can get out of here," said Isabel.

Shortly afterwards, the door opened again, and Edina entered carrying a silver tray with slices of cooked meat and buttered bread. The children had each found a book on the shelves to read while they waited. When the children saw the tray of food, they very quickly discarded the books and huddled around Edina, who sat the tray down on the desk and gave the children a big hug.

"Oh Edina!" cried Jess. "Can you help us get out of here?"

"I heard you were captured and I'm here to help in any way I can."

"Do you know what's being said out there?" asked William.

"All I know is that the King has instructed the guards to keep you here. He didn't say why, but he does seem quite upset about something."

"We had to tell him everything," moaned William.

"Everything? You mean, travelling through the trees?"

"We had no choice. He thinks we're witches!" said Isabel. "He's keeping us locked in this room until he decides what to do with us. Of course he doesn't believe us. Who would?"

"I'm not sure what I can do, but I'll try to help as best I can." Edina handed the children white linen napkins and served slices of meat in the bread.

"The King is hosting a banquet at the Queen's house this evening," said Edina.

"What does all that have to do with us?" asked Isabel.

"Well, his parties always put him in a jolly mood. He usually returns to the palace with a belly full of food and a happy disposition. He might just let you go."

The children looked at each other hoping that Edina was right.

"Now I must go, or the guards might think I'm trying to help you escape. I'll be back to see you before I turn in for the night." Edina gave the children another hug and left the room with the empty silver tray.

Later that evening, the children watched from inside the library windows as the King, dressed in his silk suit, adorned with jewels on his jacket, made his way down the steps of Kew Palace. Queen Charlotte wore a bright yellow gown adorned with diamonds that twinkled when she stepped into the carriage. Around her neck she wore pearls with an enormous diamond at the centre. Her white wig sat high on her head and she held a dainty little bag in her hand. The little princes stood at the front door and waved their parents goodbye as the carriage rode off into the distance.

An hour later, the carriage unexpectedly returned to Kew Palace. It was empty with the exception of the horsemen and a young man, who hurriedly stepped out and dashed inside. The young man ran towards Mr Dankworth. The man and Mr Dankworth began talking in the hallway and the children stood at the door and listened.

"It's the pianist!" said the man, who looked very flustered.

"What is the matter?" asked Mr Dankworth. "What has happened to the pianist? Is he injured?"

"Yes. He had been booked to play for the King and, upon stepping out of the carriage, had a fall."

"Oh dear," replied Mr Dankworth. "That is unfortunate. What am I to do about it?"

"He can't play the piano. The whole evening is ruined! Ruined! All of the King's guests travelled near and far to hear him play and now tis all ruined."

"I cannot play," exclaimed Mr Dankworth. "I am no help, nor are any of my staff, so you would do well to return to the party."

Jess's heart almost leapt out of her chest. She and William began banging on the door. "Please," she yelled. "I can help!"

Mr Dankworth ignored her, but she banged on the door even louder.

"For goodness' sake, what is it?" he yelled.

"I can play!" she squealed. "I can play piano!"

After a few moments of silence, a bunch of keys jangled on the other side of the door. The door opened and there stood Mr Dankworth, arms on hips, looking very annoyed.

"Are you telling me that *you* can actually play the piano? Are you telling me this, child?"

"Yes, sir. I'm probably not as good as the King's pianist, but if all of the guests are expecting a concert, I can do it. I've played at concerts before."

Mr Dankworth squinted his beady eyes down at Jess. "Of course you can play. All you have to do is cast a spell and you can do anything."

"Please," interrupted the young man. "The King is terribly upset. We must try something. Anything!"

"Very well then," replied Mr Dankworth. "You will be escorted to the Queen's house with the guards and return as soon as the concert has finished." Two guards escorted the children onto the carriage and off they rode.

CHAPTER 23

The eight-mile journey from Kew Palace to the Queen's house in London was a bumpy ride, for the horsemen were in a hurry, and the children bounced up and down on the seats inside the carriage. It was unlike anything they had imagined. The interior walls of the carriage were lined with a soft crimson velvet, and the seats smelled of rich leather. Embroidered cushions and a small blanket sat neatly on the floor. Isabel imagined Queen Charlotte sitting right where she was, with a cushion behind her back and the blanket over her legs to keep her warm if she needed to go to a party in the evenings. She thought of the little princes, laughing and frolicking as they would have travelled in the carriage, playing and singing as they rode through the cobbled streets of London.

Jess sat quietly thinking about what she would play. She placed her fingers on her lap and began practising. At this moment in time, she had never been so appreciative of her parents. All of the tantrums about wanting to take up dancing instead of playing the piano, all of the sacrifices her family had made in order to pay the very expensive tuition fees, all of the time they had sacrificed to watch her concerts around the country. It was now that she realised everything her parents had done for her to nurture her talent. *Wow*, she thought. *My parents are amazing.*

The carriage soon arrived at the Queen's house and stopped at an entrance inside the courtyard. Isabel was stunned when she realised they had arrived at what they knew as Buckingham Palace. Several people were waiting for them, and a butler hastily opened the carriage door and unfolded the steps. The children hopped off and were quickly ushered inside a foyer. Isabel's heart skipped a beat. "We're really inside Buckingham Palace," she whispered. "So this is what the King meant by the Queen's house."

"It's beautiful," replied William. "And it's only the foyer!"

"Come along now," came a voice. "This way." The children followed a butler through a long hallway. "Who is the pianist?" asked the butler.

"Me," replied Jess.

"Go with the footman. You will play then return to Kew."

Jess was whisked away into another room while Isabel and William were ushered into a nearby room to wait for her.

Before Jess was directed to the music room, she was handed a sheet of music by the footman. Jess surveyed the music and realised that it was a piece which was also played with a violin. She informed the footman that Isabel could join the musicians to play the violin, if there was one available. The footman summoned Isabel while butlers and servants scurried around looking for a violin. When one was found sitting on a stand in the music room, it was handed to Isabel.

When Jess and Isabel stepped into the music room, it was as though they had stepped into another world. Bright blue columns from floor to ceiling were positioned around the perimeter of the room and enormous crystal chandeliers hung from a gold ceiling. The room was full of people chatting as they sipped champagne from dainty glasses. Servants walked quietly around the room with silver trays, serving everything from quail eggs and cheese pastries to caviar and seafood. The party was in full swing with the clinking of glasses and the buzz of people chatting until a butler rang a little bell and the voices quietened down. The guests made their way over to the sofas and chairs and sat quietly in front of a gold piano.

King George stood in front of his guests and tapped his glass. The room quickly fell silent, and all eyes were looking at him.

"My dear friends," he said. "I thank all of you for coming this evening. I had a splendid evening of music planned for you all; however, my pianist has had a most untimely incident and cannot play." The guests all sighed.

"However, I am in luck, for we are fortunate to have a substitute who is able to play the piano. She is young, yes, I'll grant that, but I hear she is an excellent pianist and I'd like you to show her your appreciation in bringing your hands together for Miss Jessica Green."

King George found his seat in the front row and sat next to Queen Charlotte. He held a napkin in his hand and kept twisting it around nervously.

The guests clapped as Jess walked quietly over to the piano, scooped up her big dress and sat down. Isabel stood nearby and placed the violin under her chin. They looked at each other, and when Jess nodded, the musicians began to play. Sitting on the other side of the King was the pianist and composer for the evening, young Master Wolfgang Amadeus Mozart, with the bandage around his hand.

Jess pushed her chair in and placed her hands gently on the keys. The room fell completely silent. Her heart was pounding as the girls began to play Mozart's Piano Sonata, followed by a score they had played many times called Symphony No. 1. A little rusty at first, Jess became more confident when she noticed the King gently tapping his foot on the floor. When the girls finished the number, the guests clapped. It was a difficult symphony to get through and the girls felt every single pair of eyes staring right at them. Jess locked eyes with the King, who nodded his head in recognition of a number well played. She assumed he wanted them to play another, so they did. Jess whispered "Serenade No. 13" to Isabel and by the time they had finished, every person in the room was standing clapping their hands wildly. "Bravo," came a voice from the back. "Encore," came another. The King was jubilant, and he beamed with pride. His party was a success. As everyone continued clapping and cheering, Master Mozart walked over to Jess. She stood up nervously, wondering what he would do next. *He hated it*, she thought. *He's going to give me a telling off!* Tears rolled down her cheeks. He pulled a handkerchief from his pocket and wiped a tear from her eye.

"Ladies, you played beautifully," he said. "I wrote Symphony No. 1 quite recently and I was delighted by the fluency with which you played it, only having just seen the music on the sheet. I am not familiar with the last one you played."

At that moment, Jess realised Serenade No. 13 hadn't been written by Mozart yet.

"I don't know its name," Jess lied. "I heard it somewhere, but I'm just not sure where."

"Well, I thought it sounded marvellous. Perhaps you should consider adding cellos, violas and double base to the piece next time you play it. Shall we have something to drink?"

"Yes, please," replied the girls.

Master Mozart asked a servant for three glasses of warm milk. They sat on a sofa in the corner of the room where they chatted. When the King approached them, Jess froze, then bowed, not knowing what the proper etiquette was in the company of royalty at such a grand event.

"If I may have a word with your companion?" the King asked Master Mozart.

"Of course, Your Highness." Mozart gently bowed his head and left.

He turned to Jess and Isabel. "You have single-handedly saved my party and for that I am grateful."

"Thank you, Your Highness," replied the girls.

"Where is the young man?" he asked.

"He is waiting for us in another room, Your Highness," said Isabel.

"Find him and wait for me in the red room."

"Yes, Your Highness!"

Jess asked a butler where the 'red room' was. He placed his tray of food on a chair just outside the door of the music room and began directing Jess. "My friend William must come too," she said. "The King has asked us to wait for him."

The guard fetched William and walked them to the red room.

Upon entering the room, William said, "Now I know why they call it the red room." The big empty room was completely decorated in red. Scarlet red carpet covered every inch of the floor and red drapes hung from the windows. At the end of the room was a step which led to two giant thrones, decorated in red and gold.

"I know this room," said William. "This is where the Queen knights people."

"Which queen?" asked Jess.

"Queen Elizabeth II. I've seen it on the TV. I've seen Prince Charles do it too."

Isabel jumped onto the step. "I knight you, William Pritchard, my brother, the Duke of really awful taste in music!"

The children burst out laughing.

Then William jumped onto the step. "And I knight you, Isabel Pritchard, my sister, the Duchess of daggyness."

"Ba haa hahh!" laughed Isabel.

The children didn't hear the King enter the room, and when he said "Ahem!" they almost jumped out of their skin.

"'Tis no time to frolic," he bellowed. "For I have guests to entertain."

The children hopped off the step and bowed to the King.

"I see you are familiar with how one is knighted," he said. The children stood still, not knowing what to say or where to look.

Turning to Jess, the King said, "My dear, you are the toast of the party. You have saved me from an awfully embarrassing situation. What an inconvenience for Master Mozart."

"You are welcome, Your Highness," replied Jess.

"You are very talented. Master Mozart, too, is impressed with you and that is something to be very proud of."

Jess had never felt so proud in her entire life. To have *the* Wolfgang Amadeus Mozart be impressed with her piano playing, well, there's nothing that could ever come close to beating that.

"Now, Isabel, a serious conversation must be had," said the King sternly. "This is the second time you have helped me, and I am forever grateful. The question of what to do with you has given me much angst, to say the least. However, you are good, decent children and your duty to the Crown must not go unnoticed." He looked down at the children and placed his hand on Jess's shoulder. "Thank you for helping a king in need."

Jess beamed proudly.

The King then turned to Isabel. "Please would you stand on the step?" Isabel nervously stood back on the top of the step and an assistant pulled out a very large sword and handed it to the King.

"Kneel," he said.

Isabel thought the King was about to raise the sword high in the air and cast it down to chop her head off. In a panic, she looked over at William. Strangely he was smiling, so she closed her eyes. The King gently placed the end of the sword on her left shoulder. "I, George III, King of Great Britain and Ireland, bestow on you, Isabel..."

He glanced over at William, who whispered "Pritchard."

"Err, yes, Isabel Pritchard, Grand Duchess of Kew for saving my life as a child." He gently placed the sword on her right shoulder and stood back. "Now stand before your king."

Isabel stood up, absolutely dumbfounded.

"You are now a duchess," he said. "From here on, you shall be addressed as Isabel, Duchess of Kew and after this evening's events you and your friends will be free to go."

Isabel bowed to the King. "I am honoured, Your Highness."

"Now that you are a duchess, I think it's time you attend your first party as a duchess."

"Oh, yes, please!" The children were delighted. The King left the room with the children, and they joined the party. Jess spent most of the evening chatting to Mozart. He told her he'd just finished a tour of Europe and said his family would be returning to Vienna in a couple of days.

They discussed music, sonatas and instruments all evening. Master Mozart told Jess all about Vienna and how beautiful it was in the spring.

CHAPTER 24

A bell rang and the guests were ushered into the grand dining room where a ridiculously long table stood in the middle of the room with a hundred chairs seated around it. The table was filled with vases of beautiful flowers and every piece of cutlery had been laid out very carefully, for every knife, fork and spoon had been lined up perfectly with the next one. Crystal glasses filled the table and the guests continued chatting as they found their place card with their name and stood behind their chair at the table.

Two servants scurried into the room with three extra chairs and placed them at the opposite end of the King and Queen's chairs. When the King and Queen entered the room, everyone stopped talking and waited for His Majesty to walk to his chair. When he sat, the amulet around his neck shone brightly, which caught the attention of his guests. The King and Queen sat down then their guests sat down and the chatting resumed. At royal dinners, it was customary for the guests to speak to the person on their right during the first course, then the person to their left during the second. To the right of Isabel was a gentleman with silver hair coiffed up with a small ribbon tied together at the back of his neck. He seemed quite bemused to be sitting next to a 13-year-old, but he introduced himself anyway.

"Lieutenant James Cook," he said.

"Isabel Pritchard."

"If you don't mind me asking," he whispered, "you seem a little young to be dining with the King."

"I'm 13," replied Isabel. I have a secret. I've just had a meeting with King George III and he has made me a duchess because I rescued a young boy from drowning and saved the concert tonight when Master Mozart couldn't play."

"A duchess? Is that so?" he said, surprised. "Then I apologise, for I am required to refer to you as 'Your Grace.'"

Isabel chuckled.

"Are you here with company, Your Grace?"

"Oh yes. My brother and best friend." Isabel pointed to William and Jess, who were sitting a few seats away.

"And if you don't mind me asking," said Isabel, "what is it that you do?"

"Do?" asked Lieutenant Cook.

"Ummmm... what do you do for a living?"

"I'm a seaman. I have just finished one of my many voyages to map the coastline of Newfoundland."

Isabel had no idea that Newfoundland was the area on the very eastern tip of Canada, but she politely listened, pretending she knew exactly where it was.

"And soon I shall be embarking on a rather prodigious expedition aboard the *Endeavour* to Tahiti, where my fellow scientists and I will observe the transit of Venus across the sun. I have been appointed commander of the expedition" he said, rather pleased with himself. "This expedition will be useful for my friends at The Royal Society in allowing them to measure the solar system."

"That sounds amazing" said Isabel. "A little scary too!"

"Actually I have a secret as well" said Lieutenant Cook. "The King has handed me a secret document and given me strict instructions not to open it until after I have observed the transit of Venus. I am so keen to open it, for it's right here in my pocket."

"Oh please open it!" pleaded Isabel. "I promise not to tell what's inside."

"I cannot. It is a promise I personally gave the King."

The first course served was asparagus soup. William ate his soup slowly and managed to avoid spilling any of it. Isabel took one look at the green lumpy liquid and decided to leave it and eat the bread instead. By the time Jess had finished her first course, there were blobs of green soup all over the white tablecloth. When her bowl was collected, she covered up the blobs with her napkin. Just before the second course was served, the guests turned to the person on their left. William was astonished to find that he was sitting beside Benjamin Franklin. He had no idea until Mr Franklin introduced himself.

"Good evening to you," said Mr Franklin.

"And a good evening to you," replied William.

After the introductions, William asked, "What are you doing in London, if you don't mind my asking?"

"I am assisting the government on some important state matters."

"A secret?" enquired William.

"Yes. As a matter of fact, I spent two years in London in 1724 and rather liked it."

"I think there's a lot to like about London."

"I concur wholeheartedly."

Over the course of the evening, the conversation between William and Mr Franklin shifted from London to America.

"Much of my life has been spent in Philadelphia, where I conduct my business in printing and publishing. I then set about conducting a series of experiments in electricity. I invented a battery in which to store electricity and I discovered that there is a distinction between insulators and conductors. But alas, these days I am just a retired gentleman. I cannot be both printer and gentleman, of course. No man would be allowed that in these times."

"Some people think you're the president of America," said William.

Mr Franklin erupted with laughter. "Oh my, who on earth would think such a thing?"

William realised he had just revealed that Benjamin Franklin was often mistaken for a past president. For a moment, he had forgotten he was still in 1768.

Quickly changing the subject, William asked where he lived.

"In a fine house on Craven Street in Charring Cross. I do enjoy London very much," he went on. "It is lovely to be invited to such a fine evening."

"It is a pleasure to be sitting next to you, sir," said William.

Mr Franklin looked down at William. "You are very welcome." He smiled. "If I may be honest, it is a pleasure to be in your company too."

Mr Franklin was impressed with William's manners and thought he was quite a charming young man. He told William he very much enjoyed the music Jess played that night and if he ever bought a pianoforte, he would like Jess and Isabel to play for him.

"That's very kind of you, sir. I can speak for Jess and say that she would be honoured."

"Well then. I must get that pianoforte sooner rather than later."

After the children had finished their entree the main mean was a banquet of venison, lamb, pork and duck served with half a dozen different sauces and gravies. The butlers kept putting trays full of food on the table. When a guest's plate was empty, there was a butler on hand to fill it up again. The meat was accompanied by roasted potatoes, swede and turnips. The children were so full they could hardly sit upright. Isabel's dress felt so tight around her belly and Jess wished she was wearing jeans so she could undo the top button on them.

Half an hour after the dinner plates were cleared, dessert was served. Jellies, cakes and tarts filled the table with colour. Isabel couldn't eat anything else, but Jess took a big breath and filled her plate with everything that she could reach. After three sugared almonds and a bite of apple tart, Jess finally conceded. She was so disappointed when she looked at all the delicious food on her plate. She couldn't fit another thing inside her mouth.

When Isabel was finished eating, she slumped back in her chair and scanned the room. She heard someone laughing, which caught her attention. She peered down the end of the table and saw a middle-aged man clearly having a jolly time. As he spoke, she recognised the voice. She studied the man carefully, then all of a sudden, it dawned on her. It was John Bentley of Hanover Square. He looked older, for it was 20 years since he had first met Isabel. *Oh my goodness!* she thought. *It's John Bentley... of Hanover Square! I can't let him see me. He'll recognise me! He'll see that I'm still 13!* She ducked back against her chair when Mr Bentley appeared to look her way.

"Ahhh! Lady Gateshead!" he hollered. He got out of his seat and moved closer to Isabel's.

"My dear Mr Bentley!" replied Lady Gateshead. "What a coincidence."

"How are you? Are you well?"

"Oh, just awful, darling!" Lady Gateshead sighed. "I was watching Mr Gateshead rowing last week and I slipped and hurt my knee. Doctor said I had to lie in bed for a week! Can you imagine that? A whole week!"

"Oh, my darling," replied Mr Bentley. "How completely inconsiderate."

Mr Bentley hopped off his seat and squeezed himself next to Mr Cook, who was sitting next to

Isabel, and continued chatting to Lady Gateshead. He was so absorbed in his own conversation that he didn't even notice Isabel.

"What brings you here this evening?" Lady Gateshead continued.

John Bentley took a sip of his wine. "Tonight I am here on behalf of my father. He does commercial business with the King. Honestly, I find the whole affair so dull and tiresome that I couldn't possibly take over Father's business when he is too old for it. Why, just last week I had to attend no less than four parties in London, and it seems inexplicable that I could possibly combine my social calendar with work." After a deep breath, Mr Bentley continued. "My father really does expect far too much. In any case, my younger brother can take over the business. My social calendar calls. Oh look! There's Lady Penrith. Bye bye, dear. See you soon," and Mr Bentley hopped up again and swaggered over to the far end of the table.

Meanwhile, Isabel kept her head down and didn't dare look at Mr Bentley again. She felt exhausted just listening to him whinge about how hard done by he was. She looked over at Jess and William, who were chatting with fellow guests.

After dessert, waiters kept popping back and forth to the table to fill drinks and pick up napkins from the floor. When coffee was served, King George started to feel unwell. He began sweating and the colour quickly drained from his cheeks. A pain surged through his head and when he stood up, he became unsteady on his feet. Queen Charlotte gently held his arm, hoping nobody would notice that he was unwell. Two servants quickly came to the King's aid, and he was ushered out of the dining room through a side door. The Queen followed with her lady in waiting, who had been on standby at the door. The guests all sat around the table wondering what was wrong with the King, and before long, all manner of gossip was spreading around the table. The ladies gossiped that the King had cholera or yellow fever while the men laughed at the wild imaginations of their wives and assumed it was a simple case of the common cold. Some suggested the King had got ill over the stress of the Seven Years' War. In the King's short reign thus far, the Crown had been blighted with financial difficulties due to the expense of the war. He was not only at war with France, but with his own government ministers. At such a young age, the King was very inexperienced in dealing with such matters.

When he was undressed and tucked up in his bed that night, the amulet was removed from the King's neck. He had worn it every day since the children gave it to him. Sometimes he wore it to bed thinking it would bring him luck in every aspect of his life. How wrong he was, for the amulet did the exact opposite. He would become privy to mood swings and would often have bouts of manic incoherent ramblings.

As the King was not the rightful owner of the amulet, it was cursed and bestowed madness upon the wearer. This curse would never be broken. The children thought they had returned the amulet to its rightful owner, King George III, but they had no idea that his 60-year reign would be blighted by his gradual descent into madness. In the last 10 years of the King's reign, he was deemed unfit to rule and his son, George IV, ruled on his behalf.

The history books would remember King George III as 'Mad King George' and while professors and historians would write hundreds of books about what caused his 'madness', it was none other than the curse of the amulet.

CHAPTER 25

When the party was slowly winding down, it was time for the children to return to Kew Palace. They walked back to the courtyard where lines of carriages waited for the guests as they began spilling out of the palace, laughing and chatting, intoxicated by the most wonderful evening they had spent in the company of their beloved King George III. As each carriage pulled up, the ladies scooped up the hems of their satin gowns and hopped in, with their husbands shuffling behind them. Some gentlemen puffed on cigars as they waited for their ride home. The night air was cool, but the guests didn't seem to notice.

As the children waited for their carriage, Jess heard someone call her name.

"Jess! Jess!"

Turning around, there was Master Mozart walking towards her.

"I would like to tell you something," he said.

Mozart took her hand and shook it.

"It was an honour hearing you play this evening."

"Really? You think so?"

"You are very talented," he said. "Perhaps next time I am on tour, you might like to join me."

"Oh my gosh. I would love that!" Jess's heart leapt, then she realised she didn't belong in Mozart's time. However, the mere fact that one of the most famous composers of all time thought she was good enough to tour with was enough. She had this moment to cherish and remember for the rest of her life.

"Where can I write to you?" asked Master Mozart.

"I'll find you," replied Jess. "After all, there can't be that many Wolfgang Amadeus Mozarts in Vienna!"

"Then it is settled."

Master Mozart joined his parents, who were waiting for him. They climbed the steps and as the carriage slowly clopped away, he peered out of the window and waved to the children. Jess cheekily blew him a kiss. When he realised it was a kiss, he blushed and quickly popped his head back inside the carriage.

"I can't believe it," said a dazed Jess. "He wants to go on tour with *ME*!"

"I guess that would be like you being the backup band at a rock concert," said William.

"For the most famous band in the world," said Isabel.

"Don't ever quit piano," said William. "You don't realise it now, but you are quite brilliant. You have a gift, so nurture it."

"I will," replied Jess. "I will."

CHAPTER 26

As the children hopped into their carriage bound for Kew Palace, something rather dubious was happening behind a wall nestled next to the banks of the Thames River in southwest London.

On a small street in the suburb of Chelsea was a very special garden called the 'Apothecaries Garden'. This particular garden was created in 1673 for the sole purpose of growing plants to be used in medicine. Someone had broken into the garden and plucked plants from their flowerbeds, scraped the bark off trees and emptied them into a big sack. The following morning, the curator was aghast to find the beautifully laid gardens ripped up. Dirt covered the little paths alongside the plants, and of the surviving plants, many of them had been stripped of their leaves. When the gardeners arrived, they wept to see their little trees that were so important in the study of medicine had been ruined.

As the gardeners and local residents got together and began cleaning up the mess, a lady who lived nearby cancelled luncheon with her daughter and walked over to the gardens with a broom. She swept the dirt back onto the flowerbeds and scooped up the debris into a neat pile. Feeling tired, she sat down on the ground to catch her breath. As she placed her hand on the ground, she felt a sharp prick. "Oh!" she said and quickly jerked her hand away. Droplets of blood dripped from the palm of her hand, and she bent down to see what had cut her. A small dagger was embedded into the ground, the tip of its blade sticking up. The lady scooped the dirt away and picked it up. She brushed off the dirt and handed it to the curator, who studied it carefully. *How odd*, he thought. *This dagger looks a hundred years old.*

After a very eventful evening at the King's party, the children were exhausted. They rode silently in the carriage and by the time they reached Kew Palace, Isabel and Jess had fallen fast asleep. William gently woke them and as they hopped off the carriage, they rubbed their weary eyes.

"I'm afraid the palace is closed," said the coachman.

"It's alright." William beamed. "We're not going inside. We're going home."

"Yes, home!" Isabel yawned. "I never thought I'd be so happy to be going home."

"It's all over," said Jess. "We returned the amulet to the King and now your mum will get better."

The carriage rode off into the darkness, leaving the children standing in front of Kew Palace in the dark night. In a few moments they would be leaving 1768 and arriving in 2014, back home with their mother.

When the children arrived at their tree, William said, "Well, here we are again. Let's go home."

"Home," whispered Isabel.

"I never thought I'd be so happy to hear that word," said Jess.

Just as they placed their hands upon the trunk, a figure from the shadows bolted and flung onto the tree. William noticed the figure just as they were about to travel. "No!" he screamed. It was too late to stop. Once their hands were on the tree, there was no going back. In an instant, everyone had fallen down and landed on the grass at the base of the tree. William sat upright and to his left were Jess and Isabel. To his right stood the man who had thrashed himself against the tree.

"Who are *you*?" asked a startled William.

Before the man could answer, laughter broke out from the other side of the tree. The children recognised the laugh instantly.

"Raven?" said Isabel. "What's she doing here?"

Raven walked out from behind the tree and stood in front of the children.

"Yes! Me again!" She was clearly relishing seeing the fear embedded on the children's faces.

"Meet Osiris," she said sarcastically.

Osiris just stood at the base of the tree. He didn't say a word, for he felt worried for the safety of the children. While he was happy to laugh at Mrs Sallow's hair falling out, he was not comfortable with Raven's treatment of the children.

"Why didn't we go home?" asked William. "And why did your friend stop us from going home? What have you done?"

"Oh, I have done a lot. A lot, a lot, a lot! You see, darling nephew, while you think you're so clever with your little potion that allows you to travel through trees, I've got something much more powerful."

"And what's that then?"

"Everything! Every seed, leaf, specimen, everything from the medicine garden. I've got everything I need to make the most powerful potions ever known to man."

William knew this was very bad, very bad indeed, for Raven's power was limitless. Raven could make any potion that she couldn't previously.

"And what good will that do?" he asked. "What are you planning to do with more power? Don't you have enough?"

"Well, you know how I said I didn't need the amulet? I lied. And you're going to march right up to that house and get it back."

The children looked over to where Raven was pointing. It was Kew Palace. They had circled right back to the beginning of their journey.

"But we came here to return it!" exclaimed Jess.

"Aaaaahhhh, but you made a very grave mistake," replied Raven.

"What do you mean?" asked Isabel.

"You little brats think you know everything, that you're all so clever. The fact remains that you are children and don't know anything."

"Explain it then," said William, who was by now feeling really annoyed. "Explain why we came here for nothing."

"First of all," said Raven, "you've pretty much killed the King because he was not supposed to wear the amulet around his neck. He'll go mad now. It's already happening. When you get home and read the history books, he'll be known as 'Mad King George'. That's *your* fault! There is good power and bad power in the amulet. As you well know, when your sister and I touched it together, it gave us eternal life, but that didn't work out. But I need the amulet. I've always needed it and you gave it to that king, who will now suffer for the rest of his life."

"How are we supposed to get it now?" asked Isabel. "We can't just go into his bedroom and start rifling through his things. I bet most of the servants aren't even allowed in that room."

"You'll figure it out. You've got friends at the palace."

"Edina!" said William. "Maybe she can help."

"We can't get her into any trouble," said Jess.

"I don't think we have a choice." William sighed.

"Well then." Raven smiled. "Don't just stand here. Go!"

The children all looked at each other with dismay. As they started making their way toward the palace, something pulled Isabel back. It was as if a force was holding her back. She couldn't move her feet and so she thrust herself forward and fell over.

"What's happening?" she cried. "I can't move my feet!"

"You will stay here," replied Raven. "You are collateral."

"Izzy, it'll be alright," said William. "We'll be gone 30 minutes at most, and then we can go home. There's nothing to worry about. We've got this."

"Just trust us," said Jess.

Jess's words of encouragement made Isabel feel a little better, although she hated the idea of having to sit with Raven while she waited for Jess and William to return. She figured she'd get through it if she sat quietly and kept her mouth shut. As she watched William and Jess walk off, they soon disappeared into the darkness. When they were out of sight, she closed her eyes and thought of the beautiful music that she and Jess played at King George's party. Raven and Osiris waited under a nearby tree and Jess assumed they were discussing more wicked spells they would conjure up together. She wondered who Osiris was and how he had got mixed up with someone so evil.

It was well after midnight and the palace was quiet. Everyone was asleep, the cooks, the servants, the cleaners, Edina.

"How do we get inside?" whispered Jess.

"I'm pretty sure a palace is managed 24 hours a day. Surely there must be someone roaming around. Let's start with the doors and windows."

William tried opening the doors while Jess began with the windows. It was no use, for they were all securely locked. The wooden shutters had already been closed over the windows on the ground floor. As they made their way around the palace, Jess ran over to William.

"There's a cellar door on the other side!"

"Great!"

The children had never been around the other side of the palace, and indeed, they found a door on the ground. William gave it a yank, but it wouldn't budge. On closer inspection, he noticed a very small lock on the door. He crouched on his hands and knees looking for a rock so he could smash the lock.

"Here." Jess handed him a large rock that she found nearby. He lifted it high above his head and, with all his strength, flung it down onto the padlock. It made a small dint, so he did it again and again until the padlock flung open.

"There!" he said, feeling flushed.

"Good job!" quipped Jess.

They climbed down the stairs and found themselves in a large cellar. The only light was the moon that shone down into the bottom of the stairwell. As they walked carefully away from the stairs, it got darker and darker until it was pitch black.

"I can't see anything!" cried Jess. "It's too dark."

"Just use your hands. Feel your way around but try not to knock anything over. We have to find the stairs that lead up into the house."

William was careful feeling his way around the dark room. Most of the cellar was filled with large barrels and crates and he was thankful they would be too heavy to knock over and wake up the whole house.

Jess kept walking in a straight line until she bumped into something hard and fell over. She had stubbed her toe on the bottom of the stairs.

"I think I just found the staircase," she moaned.

"Great. I'll make my way over to you. Just keep saying *hello* and I'll find your voice."

Jess did just that and soon felt a nudge on her arm. They held hands as they carefully walked up the stairs onto a landing with a door in front of them. William squeezed hold of the handle and gently turned it. Thinking they might be in the kitchen, they were actually in a narrow corridor. They crept along the wall and stopped when they noticed a big rat scurry along the sideboard.

"Oh my gosh," whispered Jess.

"Shhhhh," said William. "It's more afraid of us."

"Disgusting."

At the end of the corridor, the children entered the kitchen, a room they were familiar with. Breathing a sigh of relief, they walked through the kitchen feeling more confident as they now knew their way around the house.

They walked to the grand staircase and stood at the bottom of it. William wondered how on earth they could pull off such an audacious plot to enter the

King's bedroom and extract the amulet from him. Would the King be wearing it around his neck as he slept? There was no way they could get it if that were the case. If it wasn't around his neck, then where would they look for it? They would most certainly wake him if they snuck around the room opening drawers, pilfering through his belongings. And what if he didn't even keep it in his bedroom? Perhaps he takes it off at night and Mr Dankworth keeps it with the rest of his jewels, such as his crown and gold rings.

William turned to Jess, and he felt as though he was going to throw up. The nervousness he felt was too much to bear.

"Jess, you must stay quiet from here on. Step quietly, walk slowly and don't say a word!"

Jess gave him a thumbs up.

William placed his left foot on the staircase and then his right. He rested his left foot on the second step, and as he placed his right foot down, the staircase creaked. A moment of panic shot through his body and he quickly stopped, his hand on the bannister and both feet on the second step. He looked at Jess and she gave him a little nod, as if to say *you can do this*. William appreciated Jess being by his side, for he knew that Isabel, being the shy little girl she is, wouldn't be able to encourage him the way he truly needed it right now. William slowly walked to the top of the stairs without making a sound. He waited for Jess, who slowly and very carefully made it to the top.

When they reached the King's bedroom door, William leaned in and placed his ear against it. It was quiet on the other side. He touched the brass door handle and gently turned it clockwise. A clicking sound made a little noise as he continued to turn the handle until he was able to turn it just enough to open the door a few inches to peer through. It was quite dark, and he could only see directly ahead to part of the curtain next to the window. As he opened the door wider, he could see the end of the huge bed that the King slept in. A little wider and the bed covers lay all tussled over a big mound. The flicker of a candle was still alight on the bedside table and William could see that the King was indeed in bed and sleeping, for he saw his chest rise and fall as he breathed in and out. The children removed their shoes and tip-toed into the room. At the end of the bed was a chaise lounge with the King's clothes on it. A dresser and chair sat under a window and a large red rug lined the wooden floor. Towards the other end of the room, two sofas sat face to face, filled with large fluffy cushions. A small coffee table sat in front of the sofas and several leather-bound folders sat neatly on top of each other.

William began with the dresser. There were four drawers, and he opened a top drawer. Surprisingly, it was empty, so he closed it and opened the second, which contained a hairbrush. Its bristles were made of horse hair and the handle was made of silver.

There wasn't anything else in the second drawer, so William bent down and opened the third, which was much bigger. It was full of papers, ink, quills, nothing that William thought was very important.

As he closed the drawer, he heard a noise from the bed. He glanced over and saw the bed covers moving. *Is he awake?* William panicked, wondering what to do. He crouched down and scanned the room for Jess. She hadn't noticed the King moving and was on the sofa looking through his folders. William couldn't whisper to Jess to be quiet and duck down as she was too far away to hear him. The King muttered a few words and rolled over. Within a few moments, he was completely still again. William opened the last drawer and there he found a small box. He gently lifted it out of the drawer and studied it. It looked expensive, for it had pictures of doves and swallows on the lid with a shiny glass exterior. He guessed it would be about 20 centimetres in diameter and had enough room to fit the amulet. Maybe this was it! Maybe this is where the King placed his amulet every night before he went to sleep. William set the box on the floor and tried opening it. To his dismay, it was locked.

"Psst," he whispered to Jess. She didn't hear him and continued rummaging around the sofas, turning up the cushions. William leaned over and grabbed the bottom of the curtain. He pulled it just enough to let the moonlight shine inside. It worked as Jess looked up and across to the window, then over at William. He put his hand up in a 'stop' motion and she quietly popped the cushion back and crept over to where William was sitting on the floor.

When she saw the box, her eyes lit up.

"We have to find the key," whispered William.

"Oh no!"

"Just look through whatever drawers you come across. It won't be under the cushions either."

"Right," said Jess, crawling away on her hands and knees.

William assumed quite rightly that the box and key would not be in the same drawer, so he looked around at the big room until he found himself looking directly at the King. He crept up to the bed on his hands and knees and stopped when he was right at the edge of the bed. William's face was centimetres away from the King and the first place he looked was around his neck, but it was bare except for the frills from his crisp white nightshirt. He glanced at the bedside table. At the bottom of the flickering candle was a mound of wax that had melted halfway down the candle as it burned away. There were no drawers in the bedside table; it was simply a round table with four legs. A book lay open on the table and William remembered being in Mrs Brown's house in Bishop's Park. He had found a key under the bedside table in the spare bedroom, so he placed his hand under the table and felt around the corners and worked his way towards the middle. No key. Despairingly, he looked up and over the bed to the other side, where he saw Jess grinning like a Cheshire cat. In her hand, she held a sparkling silver key.

"Wow!" mouthed William as he gave her the thumbs up. She slithered across the floor over to the box. She placed the key in the lock and William eagerly watched on. It was a perfect fit. She opened the box and there sitting right inside the box, adorned with cute little birds, sat the amulet. William picked it up and placed the box back inside the drawer with the key still in the lock. They hurried out of the room and tried their best to walk quietly and slowly down the stairs, but by the time they reached the bottom step, they were practically running.

When they got to the front door, they were shocked to find Edina standing there.

"What are you doing here?" whispered William.

"Please, take me with you," she pleaded.

"We can't do that! That's insane."

"I don't belong here."

"If you don't belong here, you certainly don't belong in 2014."

"But I've been there, I've seen it, and I do belong there."

Jess looked at William with the most utterly adorable puppy eyes she could make.

"No way!" said William.

"She has no family," said Jess. "Nobody will miss her. And what will her life be like here? She'll probably spend the rest of it working here, in this palace, as a servant. At least if she comes back with us, we'll be her family. She can go to school and learn, study, whatever. She will have opportunities and make a good life for herself."

"Oh gosh. Okay, okay, just hurry up. We need to get out of here."

"Yes!" said Jess excitedly.

The children, along with Edina, ran out of the front door and spilled out onto the immaculately cut lawn. They ran as fast as they could to the tree, where they found Raven and Isabel waiting for them.

CHAPTER 27

"Here's your amulet!" shouted William when he approached Raven. He then checked to see that Isabel was okay. Raven couldn't believe William had actually retrieved the amulet. She was certain he would come back empty handed with some lame excuse that it was too dark, or the King was awake, or whatever! She snatched it from his hand and clutched it against her chest. She stood there for a few moments, eyes closed, savouring the moment.

"Now it's time for us to go home, just as you promised," cried William as he crouched down and picked Isabel up from the ground.

"Edina?" Isabel was very shocked to see that she had returned with William and Jess. "What's going on?"

Jess threw her arms around Isabel. "She's coming with us!"

"Oh yes! Of course, you have to come back with us. We'll look after you."

Edina was so pleased to hear that all of her new friends were happy to take her back to their own time. She took Isabel's hands and squeezed them appreciatively. "I can't believe I'm actually leaving. I'm so happy!"

"Who's the party crasher?" interrupted Raven.

"She's coming with us," replied William. "And don't try to stop her."

"I have no interest in her. She's nothing to me."

"Let's go home," said Isabel.

"Home, home, home," echoed Raven. "Yes, you can go."

The children breathed a sigh of relief as they stepped away from Raven and walked right up to the base of their tree.

"But not you!" she bellowed.

The children looked at each other in shock.

"What?" cried Isabel.

"What do you mean?" asked William.

Raven pointed in the direction of the children. Her eyes looked wild as she said, "You three can go, but you will stay."

William quickly slapped his hand on the tree. "GO!" he shouted at the girls. "GO!"

The girls threw their hands against the tree, and all of a sudden, they opened their eyes. It was still dark, they were still at their tree, and Raven was still standing in front of them.

"What have you done?" shouted William.

"Did you think I was that stupid to let you sneak back home? I put a spell on the tree so now you can't go home together."

"Please don't do this," cried Jess. "You have the amulet. We did our bit."

"You promised," said Isabel, choking back the tears.

"Don't you know," replied Raven, "that you should never do a deal with a witch. After all I've been through, do you honestly think I'm just going to let you all get back to your perfect little lives?"

It was all too much. Jess's legs began to buckle, and she felt as though she were about to faint.

"You have exactly one minute to say your goodbyes, or I'll stop you all from going, because I'm getting tired of all this *poor me, let us go, I love you, don't go.* It's making me sick!"

William hugged the girls and drew them into a circle, all of their arms around each other.

"It's okay," he whispered. "We need to stay strong. We can come back."

"No, you can't!" Raven laughed. "There's no coming back until the white star appears in the sky."

"What white star?"

"The white star that flies through the sky. One minute left!"

"No!" Jess and Isabel hugged each other tightly and William was inconsolable as he pulled them apart. It was by far the most heartbreaking thing he had ever done, but he knew that if he didn't follow Raven's orders, none of them would be returning home.

"I'm so sorry," he said to the girls. "We have to let go."

"Please, William!" cried Isabel.

"He's right, Izzy. We have to do this. We don't have a choice."

"Ten seconds!" yelled Raven.

"Just do it! Now!" shouted William.

Edina and two of the children slapped their hands upon the tree. When they opened their eyes, they stepped back from the tree and looked around. The sun was breaking, and the light was just enough for the children to see the glasshouse on the other side of Kew Gardens. They had arrived safely back in 2014.

Three children had travelled to 1768, but one had been left behind in the clutches of Raven and Osiris.

There was no time to waste. There was no time to rest. The children had to race home and find out what Raven meant when she said *the white star appears in the sky*. The children had no clue what this could possibly mean. Which century was she referring to? Was it even in England?

CHAPTER 28

The children now had to tell Mother that one of them had been left behind. With heavy hearts, they walked through the front door of the Pritchard family home. Mother was quite shocked to see another child in her house. When the children explained who Edina was, she welcomed her with open arms.

"Edina, you can stay with us," she said. "You helped my children and for that I am eternally grateful."

"Thanking you very much, Missus," said Edina as she curtseyed. She was so accustomed to bowing and curtseying that she did it instinctively.

"There's no need for all that," said Mother. "We are all equal here." Mother squeezed Edina's hand and, when she looked into her eyes, saw a sadness etched all the way to the bottom of her soul.

Mother looked around. "Where's William?"

"There's something we need to tell you." Isabel clutched Mother's hand. Isabel and Jess told Mother everything.

"Oh my!" She burst into tears as soon as Raven's name was mentioned. "What did I do to her?" she cried. "I need my baby back! I need to go!"

"Oh, Mrs P," Jess said as she sat next to her and gave her a gentle hug. "It's not safe. You're still not better."

"She's right," interrupted Isabel. "We've just been there and if we go back on our own, we'll have a better chance."

"She said we can't get him until the white star appears in the sky. We don't know what that means," said Jess. "It must be a really big star."

"A comet!" shouted Mother. "It's a comet!"

Mother scrambled over to her iPad and manically entered her password. She searched *comets* and mumbled "*frozen gas... size of houses...*"

"That's it." Isabel placed her finger in the middle of the screen. "Halley's Comet. The last one was in 1986, but look, there was one in 1758!"

"That's got to be it," said Mother. "Says here it was the only time it appeared in the 18th century. She must have been referring to this particular date."

Mother looked sternly at the girls. "I'm going. I need to bring my son home."

"We get it," said Isabel. "I think one of us needs to stay here with Edina though. She almost freaked out seeing all the traffic on the roads. She's used to horses and carts."

"Right then." Mother grabbed her keys. "Jess, you stay with Edina, and I'll go with Isabel."

CHAPTER 29

On the way back to Kew Gardens, Mother weaved in and out of traffic and Isabel tightly clutched her seatbelt. They screeched into the car park and Isabel's thoughts came flooding back to the day of the school excursion where Jess had fallen down and hurt her ankle. If that day hadn't happened, if the school excursion had been cancelled or one of the girls couldn't go, then she wouldn't be sitting here with her mother, on their way back to the 18th century to rescue William.

Mother was in such a hurry she didn't even lock the car or pay for the parking. She ran right past the ticket machines. At the gate, she fumbled around in her bag. When she found her purse to pay for two tickets, the attendant let them straight in. "Don't worry," he said. "It's closing time soon."

Mother headed straight along the path, not entirely sure she was going the right way, for she wasn't that familiar with Kew Gardens.

"A map!" Isabel grabbed a map from the counter and pulled it apart. "We need to find a tree to take us to 1758."

"Start by looking at all the plaques under the trees," said Mother. "They should have the dates the trees were planted."

"Right, Mum. I'll go this way."

Isabel and her mother spread out in separate directions. Isabel walked past the cafe and realised how hungry she was. Her stomach would have to wait for now. A short time later, she saw her mother on another path waving at her. "Over here," she shouted.

Isabel ran towards Mother as fast as her legs could carry.

"What is it? Did you find a tree?"

"Here," replied Mother as she stood under the thick trunk of the Cedrus Libani.

"Cedar of Lebanon," Isabel read the plaque. "Looks like we found our tree."

Mother turned to Isabel and hugged her tightly. "I'll be back."

"Aren't I going with you?"

"No, darling. I need to do this on my own. My children are my responsibility and I'm not putting you in any more danger."

"But Mum," cried Isabel. "Please let me go with you."

"I've made my decision, Isabel. I'm better now that the amulet has gone, and there's something I need to do besides bringing William home."

"Okay then, I understand. I'll be waiting right here for you. Please be safe."

Mother gave Isabel one last kiss and slapped her hands against the Cedar of Lebanon. She was gone. When she opened her eyes, she was in 1758. George II was on the throne and would reign for another two years.

Mother walked around the gardens in search of William. It was getting dark, and the shadows of the trees formed eerie patches on the grass, which made visibility much harder. She knew that Halley's Comet was appearing across the sky but had no clue what day it was to happen. She was not going to wait around to find out, for it could be six months away. She stood in the middle of a clearing and closed her eyes. She began chanting:

> "Raven thine sister,
> For you I plead
> Raven thine sister,
> Come to me."

She opened her eyes and nothing. Again, she chanted louder:

"Raven thine sister,
For you I plead
Raven thine sister,
Come to me."

Just as she opened her eyes, she had a giddy feeling as though she were about to fall. She straightened up and took a deep breath. "Raven!" she shouted.

And there standing next to the tree was Raven.

"How dare you!" snarled Raven. "How dare you cast a spell to bring me here."

"I had to," replied Mother. "All I want is William. You have the amulet, so give me my son."

"Yes, I have it, but look how long I had to wait to get it."

"What are you talking about?" asked Mother.

"It was me following your kids around before they came here to return the amulet."

"What? You've been to our HOUSE?"

"Yes. I was trying to find the amulet, and when I couldn't find it, I just got bored and started playing tricks, like giving the kids a little nudge here and there."

"How *dare* you! Leave us alone. Never come back to our home again. This is your last warning."

"Or what?, What will you do? I'm more powerful. Remember that."

"Look," said Mother. "I'm just here for William. Just hand him over and we'll go."

"You can have him, but there's one last thing you have to do."

"And what's that?" asked Mother. "I'll do anything."

"I want the talisman."

"I can't," replied Mother. "I need the talisman to bring my husband home."

"Well, aren't you in a predicament." Raven smirked. "Then you must choose. William or your husband."

"Please don't do this. You are my sister, my twin. What has happened in your life to make you like this?"

"You really want to know?"

"Yes, maybe I can help you."

"Ha ha," laughed Raven. "Help me? I don't need your help. Our mother, dearest Adeline. She loved you more. You had a better life, you had nicer things than me. I had to grieve for her when she died, while you continued with your happy life."

"But our mother had to give me away because she couldn't afford to raise us both."

"But she gave *you* the amulet. Not me, but you!"

Raven stood blankly at her sister. There was no compassion, no love, just an empty soul.

"So," said Raven. "Here's what you'll do. You can have your son, but you need to return the talisman to me."

It was the worst possible scenario for Mother. If she got William back, she would lose her husband forever. And if she didn't return the talisman, she would lose William.

"Alright." She sighed. "I'll bring the talisman."

"Good," replied Raven. "Because if you don't, William will die. Now that is settled, go home and I will send William."

Mother was devastated. She watched Raven walk away until she was completely out of sight. She then turned to the tree and cried as she placed her hands upon it. When she removed her hands, she stepped back and turned around to find Isabel sitting on the grass.

"Oh Mum!" Isabel leapt up and pulled her mother in close. "Where's Will?"

"He's coming, my love."

"You're crying. What's happened?"

Mother didn't have the heart to tell Isabel she had to choose between her husband and her son. For now she would keep it to herself and try to find a way to bring David home.

"Mum! Do you hear that?"

Mother stopped and listened. The voice grew louder.

Isabel looked beyond the tree and running down the path towards her was William frantically waving his arms.

"It's Will! Mum, it's Will!"

"Oh William!" Mother ran over to William and threw her arms around him. They stood there for a very long time just hugging. Then William felt another pair of arms around him.

William put an arm around his mother and led her back to the car park. It was getting dark, and a caretaker was waiting for the last few people to leave the gardens. It reminded William of Mr Brown, the caretaker of Bishop's Park, and how he would wait at the gates every night at 8 o'clock in the evening, jangling his big ring of keys. *What an awful man*, thought William.

When Mother drove the car through the gates at the front of the house, the headlights shone into the lounge room where Jess and Edina were waiting.

"He's here!" screamed Jess when she saw William stepping out of the car.

The girls ran outside, Jess jumping into William's arms while Edina stood back with a smile beaming from ear to ear.

"You're here! I can't believe it!"

"I'll tell you everything when we get inside," said William. "But first, I have something for Edina." He pulled out a small booklet from his shirt. It was the book of names he found at Carlisle Castle. He showed the book to Edina. "Look." He flipped through the pages and there, written in black ink, were the names:

Angus Campbell,
Caitriona Campbell.

Edina burst into tears as she took the book and held it tightly to her chest. "Thank you, William," she whispered. "Thank you."

Life had to go back to some sort of normal, whatever that was for the Pritchard family. The children had returned to school and now there was Edina to consider. She hadn't been very well educated growing up and they wondered if she would like to go to school to earn her A Levels. She felt quite nervous at the prospect of sitting in a room full of teenagers, for the way she spoke and the Georgian way of life she was accustomed to would obviously draw a lot of attention. William suggested home schooling and along with Mother, they could teach her. It was a great idea and one that would earn Edina her independence and the opportunity to choose her own path in life. The Pritchards would slowly introduce Edina into the 21st century, but for the moment, Edina was happy as she was. She had her own bedroom and Isabel filled it with teddy bears and stuffed toys. Although Edina was 18 and perhaps a little old for teddies, she was grateful for the hospitality the children showed. For the first time in her young life, she finally felt like she was home.

CHAPTER 30

It was a new school day and another excursion for Isabel and Jess. This time, they were visiting the British Museum in central London. No rickety old buses in which to get bored on. They were travelling on the underground. Together the class boarded the District Line from Kew Gardens and changed to the Piccadilly Line at South Kensington. They filled up the seats in the carriage and chatted among themselves as they paired off and sat with their best friends. Of course, Isabel and Jess sat together, as they always did. They were two peas in a pod, joined at the hip, best friends forever.

The class walked the short distance from Russell Square and through the big iron gates into the British Museum. When they entered the foyer, their teacher asked them to huddle together in a group. After a quick lecture on 'do's and 'don't's, the children pulled out their clipboards and off to the exhibitions they went. On the ground floor, they viewed the Egyptian gallery as well as the Greek and Roman statues. The children were tasked with searching for various artefacts and they quickly spread out all over the museum.

Isabel and Jess made their way upstairs and found themselves in Room 41, where they discovered hundreds of artefacts in glass boxes along the walls.

"What's all this?" asked Jess.

"Looks boring," replied Isabel. "Oohh, there's a scary-looking mask over here."

Isabel traipsed over to a glass box in the centre of the room. An ancient helmet glowed under the spotlight. It was rusty brown in colour, but under the spotlight, it lit up. Two holes had been cut out for the eyes and the mask below the nose was shaped into a downward point.

Isabel began reading the plaque underneath the glass box. "Iron and tinned copper helmet... blah blah blah... Sutton Hoo ship."

"Sutton what?" said Jess.

"No, Sutton Hoo," replied Isabel. "Hoo, not what."

"I'm confused," replied Jess.

"Apparently this helmet is like a thousand years old."

"Oooohh, that's way more interesting." Jess began taking more notice of the artefacts that surrounded her. "All this stuff came from a ship that was found in Suffolk in 1939."

"What kind of ship?" asked Isabel.

"A really big one. Here it says a chamber was in the ship and a soldier was buried, but someone took his body afterwards. It also says that the soldier was Anglo-Saxon, and he was really important. All of this stuff was found in the ship that was buried in someone's garden, but there was no solider, just an empty space where he was buried. How odd."

How odd indeed. The girls had no idea that the soldier and the ship's artefacts were inextricably linked to the Pritchard family. In 600 AD, Edwin the Warrior had become Sir Edwin and, upon his death, passed the amulet to his daughter, which would be passed through the generations to Raven and Elinor's mother, Adeline. When he died, Sir Edwin's body was wrapped and placed in a burial chamber on a ship to be buried at his birthplace. When the ship sailed along the east coast of England, it ran aground just outside Ipswich. The story of the ship was a mystery from thereon, for it eventually became buried until the owner of the land had the mound excavated and unwittingly uncovered a thousand years of history.

The girls made their way back into the foyer, and within the big dome in the centre of the museum, they stumbled upon the reading room. They walked inside and sat at the rows of desks so they could complete the tasks that they had been assigned. As Isabel pulled a piece of paper from her clipboard and began writing out her notes, Jess walked over to the walls that were covered with books. She scanned the books until something caught her attention. She pulled out a folder that had 'Mozart' etched onto the spine. She opened the folder and found a sheet of music that had been carefully presented. It looked original, for the paper had turned a yellowish colour. She turned the paper over and, right down the bottom, saw a note scribbled in ink.

'My dear Jess,
I thank you for your performance in a most unfortunate circumstance.
Your dear friend,
W.A. Mozart.'

Jess's eyes lit up. She knew this letter was written for her. A librarian noticed Jess reading the sheet of music and approached her.

"Hello there."

"Oh, hi." Jess smiled.

"Do you mind?"

Jess handed the man the folder. He read the note inside. "It's still a mystery after all these years," he said, peering over the top of his round spectacles.

"What's a mystery?" asked Jess.

"See this?" The man pointed to the name *Jess*. "Nobody knows who Jess is. And we don't know what

Mozart meant by the *unfortunate circumstance.* After everything we know about Mozart, this is probably the only thing that has us all stumped."

Jess knew exactly what the note meant, but she had never seen it until now. Mozart must have tried to send it to her, but of course, she would have never received it. She wondered what adventure the sheet of music had been on to have found its home in the library room of the British Museum in the 21st century. She hurried over to Isabel with the folder.

"You won't believe this..."

"Won't believe what?"

Jess handed Isabel the folder. "Open it."

Isabel slowly opened the folder.

"Oh, hurry up! I'm bursting."

Isabel glanced at the sheet of music.

"No, silly. Turn it over."

Isabel turned the sheet over, and as she read the note, her eyes lit up.

"Oh my goodness. You're *the* Jess."

"I know! The librarian said nobody knows what the note means."

"This is amazing," said Isabel. "You and I are the only people in the whole world who actually know that you are *the* Jess and what the note means."

"Shall we keep it that way?"

"Absolutely! Nobody would believe us anyway."

"But what about Mum and William? Shall we tell them?"

Jess thought about it for a few moments. "Nah. It will be one of our many secrets."

"Best friend secrets."

On the way home, Jess sat on the tube and thought how lovely it felt to have had such a special friendship with one of the greatest composers in history.

When Isabel returned home from school, it was time for Mother to sit down with her children and tell them they had to hand the talisman over to Raven. Now the family had two problems. They had to deliver the talisman to Raven, or she would come for William and make him disappear forever. And what of the key that Raven had in her possession? Raven told William it opened a chest that contained a very special book. The question was, where was the chest?

THE END

Lightning Source UK Ltd.
Milton Keynes UK
UKHW012354230822
407651UK00002B/117